For Mum, Dad and Edward,
Thanks for always being there. You guys are the best.

Lily Blake is a twelve-year-old, whose
she finds both exciting and troublesome.
transferred...                          and Peace Insurance...

Lily Blake

# THE ELEMENTS – I

## The Heroes' Journey

AUSTIN MACAULEY PUBLISHERS™

LONDON • CAMBRIDGE • NEW YORK • SHARJAH

A CIP catalogue record for this title is available from the British Library.

ISBN 9781398431089 (Paperback)
ISBN 9781398431096 (ePub e-book)

www.austinmacauley.com

First Published 2022
Austin Macauley Publishers Ltd®
1 Canada Square
Canary Wharf
London
E14 5AA

Firstly, thank you to everyone at Austin Macauley Publishers for giving me this opportunity and making my dream a reality.

Thank you to all my favourite authors who wrote magnificent books: Cressida Cowell's *How To Train Your Dragon* and *The Wizards of Once*, Rick Riordan's *Percy Jackson, Heroes of Olympus and Trials of Apollo*, Eoin Colfer's *Artemis Fowl* and S.F Said's, *Phoenix* (in my opinion, the best stand-alone sci-fi novel there is at the moment), Phillip Pullman's, *Mortal Engines*. There are so many authors who have, and continue, to inspire me.

Thank you to my little brother, Edward, who says he is my number one fan already, and I totally believe him. Almost every day, I will receive some sort of drawing under my door that promotes this book. *Elements Rule – I* is a popular slogan of his.

And thank you to everyone else who isn't on this list but has shown me support through reading the manuscript at various stages and offering advice.

# Prologue

Two children, a girl and a boy, were standing in a graveyard. Both were wearing black, and both had red eyes from crying. The girl was gazing at the sky.

'Rick, do you think they're watching us?' she said, looking at the boy.

No reply. She undid her bright red hair and let it flicker like a flame in the breeze.

'What are we going to do now, Rick?'

Rick looked at her, his eyes shining. She didn't know what it was from; tears or determination. He stared at the girl for a while, running his fingers through his curly hair.

'I don't know, Gwen, I don't know.'

# 1. Best-Friends-Who Live-With-Each-Other

Gwen wasn't listening. She generally didn't in science. Who actually cares about friction or space-time continuum or Newton's apple? Gwen certainly didn't. Luckily, she had a method that saved her the whole bother of listening to Mr Watson blathering on.

'Gwen,' he said, uncertainly. 'Could you please tell me— um, what are you doing?'

Gwen smiled. She loved the way she could creep people out just by looking at them with her huge golden eyes. She didn't care that people thought she looked like her head was on fire, what with it being a bright shade of auburn. In fact, she positively enjoyed it.

'I'm not doing anything, sir,' she replied with a grin. 'But why are *you* staring at me?'

'Never mind. Anyway…'

The class burst out laughing. It had worked. Again. She had got out of at least three major embarrassments by doing this. And it worked for everyone. Except one person. She would never ignore that one person anyway. He was the most important person in her life.

The lesson dragged on and on while Gwen daydreamed. She did this to stop herself from thinking about *that* thing. The thing that had happened to her parents. They had died in a car crash two years before and she had been living with another family ever since. She felt tears pricking her eyes as she thought about it. Gwen silently cursed herself. She cursed Skoda. And she cursed roads.

Finally, after what seemed like forever, the bell rang for the end of the day. She hoped that she wouldn't have to wait too long. Gwen stood outside the school until she saw who she was waiting for. Fredrico Brown. He was the son of her adoptive parents, and so, technically, was her brother, but they preferred to think of themselves as 'best-friends-who-live-with-each other'. Gwen couldn't help staring at Rico's long, curly black hair and his pointy face and ears. She felt a little bad, but she thought he looked very pixy-ish.

'Hey,' he called, as he strolled over to Gwen. He looked absolutely exhausted. *No wonder,* she thought. *He had Ms Daniel.*

'Sorry, I took so long. Ms Daniel still has a habit of ignoring the bell, even after two years of being here,' he said, rubbing his eyes.

'Yeah…she does.' Gwen shuddered to think about it.

'Good Lord, Mum's going to kill us if we don't get back soon.'

'Shall we run?'

'I am *so* gonna win!'

Gwen laughed. *Not likely,* she thought. She had been practising during PE.

It turned out that Gwen would have to practice a whole lot harder next time in PE. They ran through the streets pushing

11

past old ladies, grumpy teens, and a small girl who looked lost. Someone even threw a newspaper at her.

'Sorry!' she yelled, though she didn't really mean it. She was too busy trying to keep up with Rico. Despite Gwen being totally out of breath and mortally embarrassed, they turned up at Rico's house in no time.

'Hate to say I told you so, Gwen, but – I told you so!' said Rico, giving her a smug grin.

'Oh, very funny,' she replied, frowning. 'I bet I'll finish your mum's pesto pasta quicker than you, though.'

Gwen laughed inside. Rico's mum was Italian and was obsessed with making her family eat Italian food. Rico's older sister, Zoe, absolutely loved it, while Rico could only try his hardest not to gag and retch while eating it.

'Yeah,' he said, miserably. 'I'm sure you will.'

As they unpacked their bags in the hallway, Gwen couldn't stop herself twirling around and staring at all the ornate Italian pottery that Mrs Brown had brought back from her home country. There were so many different colours: rubies and oranges, cornflower-yellows and emeralds, azures and violets. They were in so many different shapes and sizes that Gwen couldn't keep a count. She absolutely loved the Brown's house. An interesting house for an interesting family. She couldn't help but think about her parents. Maryanne and Richard Northe. She remembered her house being extremely dull. The only fun things there were the photos of Gwen and her parents surfing. Her mum was ace at it. Gwen's train of thought led her to something that had been nagging her for the past two years. In all the photos she had in her room, her parents would stand on either side, and Gwen herself would sit grinning in the middle. But there would always be a space next to her as if her parents were waiting for someone. Or as if someone was missing…

'Gwen? Gwen?' Someone was calling her name. 'Earth to Gwen, do you read?'

She was jarred back to the present by Rico engaging her in their small running joke. Gwen was famed for daydreaming.

'Loud and clear,' she said trudging into the kitchen. 'Just a little…'

'Roger that,' said Rico sitting down at the table next to her. 'But seriously, what's the matter? We don't want our little space shuttle *Gwen 13* crashing into the monstrous asteroid known only as *Zoe,* do we?'

That earned him a withering stare from his sister who had chosen that moment to walk into the room.

'Excuse me?' she said, glaring at her younger brother. Being fifteen, Zoe did this a lot. 'If *anyone's* the asteroid, it's Dad.'

'Hey!' cried Mr Brown from his position in the living room watching football. 'I heard that!'

'You were meant to!'

Zoe left it at that and went to eat a piece of stray cheddar cheese that was lying on the table.

'You are…absolutely disgusting,' muttered Rico. 'I don't know how you do it.'

But Gwen wasn't listening. She was too busy staring at the ginormous plate of food that had just been put in front of her.

'*Ecco che, mia cara,*' said Monita Brown, beaming as she dished everybody a portion that was big enough for an elephant. Gwen didn't have a clue what Monita had just said, but she knew enough to say thank you.

'*Grazie,*' she said, poking at her food. Gwen wasn't really hungry.

'You are most welcome, Gwendoline dear.'

Gwen froze. Mrs Brown was the only person who called her by her real name. Everyone else knew she hated it but she didn't have the heart to tell Monita that.

Gwen stared at Rico. He looked like he'd seen a ghost. Even more so than usual.

'You're not gonna be sick, are you?' said Zoe, wrinkling her nose. 'Because if you are, then get the heck out of here.'

Rico stared at his sister. Gwen saw a look pass his face that she'd never seen before.

'Excuse me,' he said then left the table and stomped upstairs. She wondered what the matter was with him.

After they had finished their (extremely) delicious dinner, Mrs Brown called Rico down and made the whole family squeeze onto the three-seater sofa in the living room. There was nowhere near enough room but Monita insisted. *Family night* was very important to her. Unfortunately, each person had their own definition of the phrase.

'Hey!' yelled Mr Brown for the second time that day. 'I was watching the football!'

'Darling, you have been watching the football for three hours,' said Mrs Brown rolling her eyes at her husband. Rico was squished in next to Gwen.

'Family night, my toe,' he whispered.

Zoe had decided to put on her favourite talk show: *Little Stars*. They interviewed child stars though many of them said they should be on the adult programme. Children like *The Little Madam* that was on there now.

'Is that Bethany Hill?' asked Rico. 'My God, she's cut her hair.'

It was Bethany Hill, daughter of the famous actor, Manfred Hill. She had been forced into the acting business and positively hated it. She hated that she was treated like a child even though she was fourteen. And she hated her father. Gwen only knew this because Bethany had stated it in public. The host was obviously picking up on Bethany's bad mood and was trying to make light conversation.

'So, Bethie,' she said, nervously. 'How did the new movie go?'

Bethany glared at the host with her startling blue eyes. If looks could kill, the host would be long gone.

'I have to admit,' said Bethany, in her cold American voice. 'Not very well. I tell you this every time, Moya, it never goes well for me. That's why as soon as I turn eighteen, I'm gonna leave this business.'

Moya started. 'Excuse me?'

'I said, as soon as I can, I'm going to leave this business.'

'Oh.'

Rico's dad did not look impressed.

'What an obnoxious little princess!' he exclaimed. 'Could somebody please turn this nonsense off the TV?'

And that's how they ended up watching FA cup highlights till ten. By then, Rico and Zoe had already cleared off, but Gwen didn't want to hurt Mr Brown's feelings.

'Um, I'm a little tired, I'll go up to bed now…' she said, hesitantly. Monita was asleep on the sofa and Mr Brown was transfixed to the TV. No one heard her so she slipped upstairs.

Gwen wasn't *really* tired. She just said that to get away from the living room and be alone for a bit. To think. About *the thing.* She picked something up from her bedside table. It was a small ring in the shape of a miniature flame. She had found it on her bed this morning and had been very puzzled because she hadn't seen it before. It looked like one half of a Yin and Yang symbol. Gwen wondered where the other half was.

It took Gwen a long time to drift off, she was just closing her eyes to the sound of the clock striking twelve when she saw a light flicker across the hallway outside her open door. She got out of bed and peeked outside. Okay, no one to the left. And—wait. Rico's light was on. What was that all about? According to Rico himself, he slept like a log. Gwen creeped along the passage, the wooden floorboards quietly creaking underneath her feet. The walls were adorned with beautiful paintings of the Italian countryside. Gwen sighed. It was at times like this that she wished she lived in Italy.

She made it to Rico's door. A tiny slither of light was flickering from the electric candle he kept on his bedside. It was midnight. Why wasn't he asleep? Then again, she wasn't. Gwen took a deep breath. Should she go in or not?

# 2. The Rings

Rico was standing in the school library, trying not to look suspicious. He wanted to go to the family history section, he had always been interested in that. Even though Ms Daniel was his History teacher. It had been on his mind ever since Gwen moved in with him. She hadn't mentioned anything about her family and Rico was curious, but it had escaped his mind to check. So, he was doing it now.

Rico wandered through the bookshelves. You wouldn't know it by looking at him, but this is where he felt right at home. In between the pages of a book, deep inside a library, where nobody would ever find him. He picked up a book saying *Tippinham Family History*. That was what he was after. He looked through the contents. 'N' was on page 114. His house number. He flicked through until he found *Northe*. Rico didn't actually know if she would be in here, he was just assuming Gwen was from Tippinham, too. He looked at the careful illustrations. Two people were at the top of the page; a man called Richard and a woman called Maryanne. That was a nice name. He looked down and sure enough, there was Gwen, the drawing only slightly less beautiful than she was. But something was wrong. There was somebody else next to her, a boy named Rick. Gwen hadn't said anything about having a brother. He looked a lot like Rico. How odd. He then flicked back to 'B' where his father's family joined with his mother's. Monita and Carl. He looked down and there was Zoe. So far so good. But something was wrong with this one too. He wasn't there. Had this been made before he was born? No, because Rico and Gwen were the same age and she was in there. He would have pondered longer but the caretaker had come in and was eyeing him evilly. He checked the book out at the counter and decided to think later.

Rico and Gwen had their lunch in the hall as usual. It had been absolute mayhem. Tommy Wilson had decided to throw a ham sandwich at his mate and obviously that had developed into something much, much worse. Rico didn't want to even *think* about the details. Let's just say that the cleaners had a very big job on their hands. They would have to call in an entire cleaning squad. A hygienic army. After they had been through the trauma of the cafeteria, they went to lessons. Rico had Ms Daniel for double History (yippee) and Gwen had Art and then, Science. She didn't like either of those.

'Meet me outside!' she called as they parted ways.

'Try not to kill anyone out of boredom!' he yelled back, heading to the Humanities Corridor.

History dragged on as usual. They were doing the battle of Hastings which, if you were Mr Wright, would be very exciting and full of people acting out the battle. But he did not have Mr Wright. He had Ms Daniel. And she never told you the fun, gory things. She just told you: dates, facts, places and more dates and facts. She then made you write a mini essay for the lesson. Rico couldn't help but think *we're in Year Eight for goodness sake. Give us a break.* He didn't say that, but Gary Withers had said something similar and a lot, lot ruder two months before. Gary Withers wasn't at this school anymore.

'Class,' said Ms Daniel in her weird nasally voice. 'I would like you to write an essay on the Battle of Hastings using the information on the board.' The whole class groaned. It wasn't as if they didn't know what was coming. They just didn't want to do it.

'And,' she carried on. 'If anybody refuses it will be detention for everyone.' Thirty pairs of round eyes stared at her.

"*Everyone.*"

And so began the start of one of the most boring lessons in Rico's life. He finished about three quarters of the way through so he had to sit in uncomfortable silence and stare at the timeline on Ms Daniel's wall for at least half an hour when he was finished. At least, that gave him a chance to think about the book from the library. Why was that boy next to Gwen? And why was he not there? And why—?

'Rico Brown.'

'Yes, ma'am?'

'Why are you not working?'

'I've finished, ma'am.'

'Well check your work again then!' Rico did not want to *check his work again then*. He had already done this ten times. He knew because he had counted. Nevertheless, he made a big show of turning over the pages; picking one up so it rustled and slamming it (quietly) onto the table so everybody flinched. In the end, Ms Daniel said 'You can stop checking now, Rico.' which gave him the indication he had won that particular battle. Unfortunately, it still didn't give him any time to think because no sooner had he put his folder down, the bell went. Ms Daniel didn't do anything to show she had noticed it, so little Riley Budd spoke up.

'Ma'am?' she said.

'What?'

'Um, well…'

'Get to the point!'

'The bell's gone!' Ms Daniel looked at the clock.

'So it has…' she said. 'You could've been more polite, Riley. Hmph. Off you go then.' Nobody needed telling twice.

Rico rushed off to find Gwen standing outside already.

'Hey,' he called, strolling over to her. 'Sorry, I took so long. Ms Daniel still has a habit of ignoring the bell, even after two years of being here.'

'Yeah…she does.'

'Good Lord, Mum's going to kill us if we don't get back soon.'

'Shall we run?'

'I am *so* gonna win!'

And so they ran home; Rico in the lead and Gwen wheezing behind him. They arrived at his house in no time and Gwen was just as stunned by the decor as she always was. He wasn't really concentrating but he could see she was upset about something. He tried to make her laugh by calling her a space shuttle like they did when they first met. It didn't work. And then Zoe (that monster) thought he was going to be sick! She just couldn't get her head around the fact that he was naturally pale. So, he stalked off. Not the best manners but *oh well*. Zoe's weren't exactly in prime condition either.

Rico was called down at seven so he could participate in *Family Night*. He could honestly say he saw no point whatsoever in doing it because, quite frankly, nobody wanted to. The only reason he stayed down at all is because he knew his dad had been watching the football and Zoe would not put up with that. In fact, the minute she sat down, Zoe groped around for the remote control (or *doofa* as his dad liked to call it) and immediately switched on *Little Stars*. Rico normally couldn't stand the little morons that went on that show but he could put up with Bethany Hill. She hated it and so did Rico. He was willing to watch it because of that.

Unfortunately, his dad couldn't stand it, whether it had Bethany on or not, so he turned the "nonsense" off. Rico decided he would much rather mope around in his room than watch a bunch of middle-aged footies reminisce about "the old days", so went upstairs and shut the door.

He rummaged around in his school bag until he found what he was looking for: the family history book. Rico wanted to look at both pages simultaneously so he took a photo of each of them and printed them out. He then laid them on his bed and twiddled the little ring he had found on his bedside table that morning. It was shaped like a water droplet and was curved like it had another half. He wondered who had the other one. Staring at the two pages, he was escorted to a thought that had been bothering him for a while now. He wasn't in any of the family photos. And he was pretty sure it wasn't because Mum and Dad didn't like him, even though that might be the case with Zoe. He gazed at the two pages; you could almost hear the gears inside his brain ticking away. Suddenly, it hit him. He knew why Gwen had another sibling and Zoe didn't have any. Rick. Rick-o.

'Rico?'

He started and turned to face the door.

'Aahh!' he whisper-shouted. 'Oh, it's only you, Gwen. Could you please not do that again? I nearly wet…'

'Alright, I get the picture,' muttered Gwen, grimacing. 'Anyway, why aren't you off in the land of nod right about now?'

'Why aren't you?'

'Good point. I can't sleep. You know, I can't. What's that?' said Gwen, pointing to the book pages on his duvet.

'Oh, them…' said Rico, his heartbeat increasing. He took a deep breath. 'Gwen, there's something I need to tell you.'

'Go on.' She looked at Rico with her intense golden eyes. He felt himself gulp.

'You said that there are spaces in your family photos.' Gwen looked surprised.

'How did you know that?'

'You told me.'

'Oh yeah. Sorry. Carry on.'

'And, you know, how I'm not in any of mine? Well, I think I know the answer.'

'Yeah?' whispered Gwen.

'Well, it's just a theory but…I think you may or may not be my sister.'

'Ohhhkayyy…Explain.'

'See for yourself.' Rico showed her the paper. She looked like she was going to faint there and then.

'Holy mother,' she murmured. 'But your name isn't Rick.'

'I know,' said Rico. 'But it would make sense wouldn't it?'

'I guess it would. Well, at least that's the photo mystery solved.' she said, sighing. But Rico wasn't done yet. He looked up at her from the bed.

'There's just one more mystery. Have you seen,' he asked, picking up the ring, 'anything like this before?' Gwen looked even paler than he was.

'Hold that thought,' she said, getting shakily up from his bed and padding down the hallway. Rico was beginning to think he'd scared her off when she reappeared in the doorway, her fist clenched around something.

'Look,' she said, her voice barely audible. Rico opened his eyes. He began to feel how Gwen looked.

'They're…' he couldn't even finish his sentence. So Gwen finished it for him.

'The same,' she said. 'No, not quite the same. Mine is a flame and yours is a—what is that? A water droplet?'

'Yeah. Yes, it is. They look like they're meant to go together. Should we—?' Gwen replied instantly.

'Yes.' And so they did. They put the Yin and Yang symbols together. Rico braced himself. He was right to. Because as soon as the rings touched each other, a bright burst of purple-black light bathed the room. It looked like a sort of hologram you saw in *Star Wars*. He was right about that part. It was hard to tell but it looked like there was a figure appearing through the light. The static made it hard to tell but Rico was pretty sure it was a girl. A girl who would've been at least two metres tall if she was real.

'If you are watching this then you must have figured it out,' said the girl, her long gauzy hair floating around her head.

'I presume you are the Northe twins. I must say, I'm glad you found each other. My partner wanted to split you up; he thought you would be too powerful as a pair. I secretly hoped that fate would bring you together and sure enough it did. But let me tell you who you are first. And whatever you think, I want you to believe it. I assume that you have heard of the elements; fire, water, air, earth and ice. Well, you are two very important elements. One is fire and one is water. You won't have any memories of it now, but they should come back soon enough. Anyway, I need you to follow these instructions very carefully. I have chosen you to be the finders of two of the other elements; air and earth. Don't worry about ice, we already know of him. You must travel to Tippinham Moor when it is covered in mist, there you will find Air. Then, you must go to the Carmin Woods, there you will find Earth. As soon as all four of you are assembled, I want you to meet me at the ghost town just south of here. There, I will brief you before we make our way to the Mansion of Night where you will begin your training. Your parents trusted you and so do I. Because not only do the elements need you, the Planet needs you. I warn you, it is a dangerous life but as I said before, I trust that you will accept it. You have a week to find the others. I hope to see you then.'

The hologram disappeared. There was a few minutes of stunned silence, until Gwen spoke up. 'Okay, I just witnessed that,' she managed, staring deep into her brother's eyes. 'Who the heck was that weird lady?'

'I don't know,' said Rico, his breath ragged. 'But you heard what she said. Tomorrow, we pack our bags and go to Tippie Moor.'

'Two things. What about your par—I mean the Browns? And also, isn't Tippie Moor meant to be really dangerous? Even when there isn't any mist?'

'Yes, it is, but where else are we meant to go? And I'm sure the Browns won't even remember who we are.' Rico suddenly felt dizzy. A waterfall of images flooded into his mind and filled in all the holes that had been made in his brain. He looked up.

'Gwen,' he asked weakly. 'Did you just get mind-mugged by your memories?' Gwen looked equally as awful as himself.

'Yep,' she said taking long, deep breaths. 'Well, if we're going to Tippie Moor tomorrow, we should probably get some sleep.' And with that she staggered out of the bedroom rubbing her eyes. Rico doubted he would get any sleep after that but he lay down and closed his eyes. He had found out the entire truth in less than an hour. He now had a twin sister, two parents (even though they were dead) and a very busy future to look forward to. And the best thing was, he could now remember everything. All the memories of Gwen and him, when they were little, fitted nicely into place where he could remind himself that he wasn't alone in this crazy adventure…

# 3. The Mist of Tippie Moor

'I hate taxis,' was Gwen's opening line when Rico told her what mode of transport they would be using to get to Tippie Moor. She now knew *why* she hated taxis; when she was four years old, a taxi driver had a particularly gruesome scar on his forehead. That very same taxi driver had told her not to mess on the road or the same would happen to her. She hadn't been in a taxi since. Unfortunately, this was the only mode of transport they could afford. Especially if they wanted to get to the Carmin Woods afterwards, with their new friend. Gwen still could not believe last night's events had really happened. She kept instructing Rico to pinch her arm until she had a bruise.

'I'm gonna stop now,' said Rico. 'Or someone's bound to accuse me of abuse.' That didn't seem likely, though, because when they went downstairs with their bags to wait for the taxi, Gwen said, 'Bye Zoe. Bye Mr and Mrs Brown. I'll miss you.' And they didn't even flinch. Even though Zoe was staring straight at her with her long brunette hair plaited over her shoulder. It was like they didn't even know the elemental twosome were there.

'I bet you anything, it's that weird lady,' said Rico. 'She's probably wiped their minds or something.' Even though,

Gwen had only known the Browns for two years, she still felt a twinge of sadness as she closed the door and posted the keys back through the letterbox. She might have her brother back, but the Italian themed house had been her home for the past twenty-four months. Gwen really was going to miss them.

'Come on, Little Miss Emotional,' called Rico from the taxi that had just pulled up outside. Was she really ready to embrace the epic adventure before her? To become an actual real-life heroine with superpowers and save the world? Gwendoline Northe decided then and there that she would do anything as long as it was with her brother.

She climbed into the taxi's back seat beside Rico. Luckily, the driver was a young woman and she did not have a humongous, ghastly scar across her forehead.

'Where are we going then, lovies?' Gwen let Rico do the talking. Grown-ups usually got quite agitated when you told them you were going to Tippie Moor. She was right.

'We'd like to go to Tippinham Moor, please,' said Rico, in his best cutesy voice. Maybe the cutesy voice was a bit much. The driver appeared to think they were two years old.

'I'm afraid I can't take ya' there,' she said. 'It's proper dangerous.' Fortunately, Gwen was thinking on her toes.

'Yes, but our Grandma lives in a cottage not far from there,' she said giving the driver the full extent of her round golden eyes. 'And there aren't any more taxi stations.' Maybe the cutesy theme wasn't so bad. The driver certainly seemed to buy it.

'Alrighty then. Just you be really careful, won't ya?' she said, sliding the compartment partition closed.

'We will,' they chorused, sounding for all the world like a miniature school choir. After Rico was sure that the driver couldn't hear them, he leaned over and whispered, 'What was all that about? You made us sound like flipping Red Riding Hood and her new counterpart Rico Red Riding Hood.' He looked at Gwen and grinned. He had decided to keep his name as Rico because if he changed it back to Rick (short for Richard by the way) then who knows what they'd call him at school. If they even went to school after this.

Gwen grinned back at him and said 'Well, Red Riding Hood isn't flame resistant, is she?' Gwen had a quiet chuckle. This morning, to put her supposed powers to the test, Gwen had figured that if she was the Fire element she would therefore be flame resistant. She then stuck her hand in the fireplace which was crackling away merrily. Luckily for her, she was fireproof and was determined to rub Rico's nose in it for all eternity. However, Rico had vowed that as soon as they found a decent sized body of water, he wanted to find out if he could breathe while submerged. Gwen had protested that he could kill himself but apparently it was only fair that he could have that power if Gwen was fireproof. She supposed Rico was right.

The taxi pulled up outside a rather depressing little wooden shack that Gwen assumed was meant to be the taxi station. It looked like it hadn't been used in decades.

'Alright lovies,' said the driver, turning to face them. 'That'll be twenee quid if you don't mind.' Gwen looked at Rico who was pulling a note out of his wallet. A wallet that Gwen had got him on their eleventh birthday. Their last birthday as twins. She looked at him closely. *Anything with Rico*, she thought, opening the door. Here we go. This is the start of something bigger than anything she'd ever known. They thanked the driver and stared at the ominous fog that lay before them. A fog that went on seemingly forever. The taxi drove away leaving a trail of fumes in the cold morning air.

'I presume that that is the Mist of Tippie Moor,' said Rico flicking a water droplet off his jacket. 'Doesn't look very appealing, does it?'

Rico was right. The fog loomed over everything, devouring anyone stupid enough to actually go there. *That makes three of us,* thought Gwen. *Me, Rico and the other one.* She wasn't sure why she had agreed to do this. Tippie Moor was famous for being riddled with holes and crevices just lying there for anybody to walk into. And it was worse with the mist; you couldn't even see where you were going. Which is *exactly* why they were going there. A real no-brainer on their part.

'If we die here,' said Gwen, stepping over a particularly marshy patch of ground. 'Who's gonna sue that weird lady?' Rico smiled at her.

'One: we're not going to die here. And two: maybe the Air element could? They're in here somewhere, aren't they? It's not like they're going to wait forever. Or maybe they will. Who knows.'

'Who knows,' she replied miserably. This was quite possibly the worst idea she had ever come across. Couldn't that lady have told the Air element to wait somewhere different? Preferably somewhere safe that wasn't notorious for making people disappear from the face of the Earth? She obviously had bad taste when it came to heroic venues. Gwen listened hard. The only sound she could hear were birds calling to each other in the distance. There was another sound too, or maybe it was just Gwen hearing things. She thought she could hear someone other than Rico breathing…

'Hold up!' yelled Rico, and just in time, too. Gwen had almost stepped into one of those infamous craters. *Note to self*, she thought, dusting herself off. *CONCENTRATE*. She had no desire to become a flat Gwencake.

'Thanks,' she managed.

'You're welcome. I figured you didn't want to be a…'

'Flat Gwencake? Yeah. I mean, no I don't.' She stared at the sky. Or the fog. There was no sky to stare at. Gwen shook her head and carried on after Rico. This time, she was careful to look at the horrible, boggy ground as she walked. She wondered whether the Air element actually was in here. If they were, *where* were they? As much as Gwen resented the idea of venturing deeper into Tippie Moor, she couldn't hide her excitement at meeting someone new. All her life, her only friend had been Rico. And *she* had been *Rico's* only friend. It would be a nice change to be around a different person for once.

'Hey Gwen,' came Rico's voice from somewhere in front of her. 'Are you seeing this?' Gwen couldn't see anything but endless fog.

'Seeing what?' she asked.

'That thing over there.'

'What thin—oh. Yeah. I see it.' She squinted into the mist. Gwen could just about make out a hazy figure sitting on some rocks. Could it be what they were looking for? There was no way to tell unless they went closer.

'Um, Rico? You wanna go see who that is?'

'Not really.'

'But…But you have to.'

'Well then we'd better go over there then.' Gwen tried her best to spot Rico through the fog. When she did eventually find him, she glared at him.

'*We?*'

'Yes, Gwen. We do this together. Now, come on. I'm sure they're harmless.' Gwen snorted at him in her mind. Nothing in Tippie Moor was harmless. Okay, maybe the tall grass was harmless but that wasn't the point. Gwen rolled her eyes and trudged over to Rico. As they got closer to the figure, she could make out more and more details. The person wasn't sitting on a rock, they were perched on a backpack and two handheld carrier bags. And the person was a girl. Wearing…Were they Scooby Doo scrunchies? *Oh jeez*, she thought. *I have my doubts.*

'Hello?' said Rico, walking over to her. She had the wildest, frizziest hair that Gwen had ever seen and skin the colour of coffee beans. She looked like she had been waiting for a *long* time.

'I'm Rico,' Rico carried on. 'And this is Gwen. What— what's your name?' The girl raised her head, slowly.

'I—' she began and then thought better of it. She decided to take a quick identity test first.

'Did you get a hologram with a weird lady on it?' she asked. Gwen smiled. This girl wasn't so bad. They were definitely on the same wavelength.

'Yes.' Gwen replied. 'Are you the Air element?' This time the girl smiled back.

'A 'yes' from me, too.' she said, grinning. 'And my name's Sky.'

# 4. Sky

Sky wasn't what you would call a 'cool kid'. She had short, frizzy, out-of-control hair that her siblings teased her for and she wasn't into the same stuff that her sister was in to. Quite the opposite. On the particular evening that she had received the hologram of a weird lady with much better hair than she had (long story: the hologram had come from Sky's earrings) Sky had been in a sulk. Her sister, Sandy, had just criticised her style. Sandy took a lot of pleasure out of doing this.

'Hey, Sky,' she had said, smirking at her younger sibling. 'Why are you still in your PJs?' Sandy knew very well that Sky wasn't in her "PJs" but they did look like something you might wear to bed. Jeans with holes in the knees and a vest top with a big "S" on it would not be your regular thirteen-year-old girl's choice of clothing. But Sky wasn't regular. She was small for her age, she had no friends, she wore blue-rimmed round glasses that her brother Mo called "Nerd Specs" and, of course, she was the element of Air.

By the time Sky had thought up of a cunning reply to her sister's sarcasm, *'And why are you wearing a Halloween mask in March?'*, Mo had walked into the room and was joining in the fun. Mo was nearly three years younger than her but had way more friends and was way more popular. Sky tried not to take offence at this fact but it was hard to ignore your ten-year-old brother dancing around your feet singing "Sky has Nerd Specs, Sky has Nerd Specs!" in a silly singsong voice. She was a placid girl in general, but this had been going on for several months now, ever since she had got her glasses. Sky had wanted a pair of cheap ones so she could pay for them herself but her mother, Sara, had said, 'Your father makes all this money in America, and you don't even want to spend it!' Sara had then proceeded to buy Sky the most ridiculous, moronic specs that she had ever seen. Sky sometimes wished her dad hadn't gone over to America. What was the use in working for Microsoft if you didn't even get to see your kids? Bruno, Sky's dad, had only come over to England to visit once last year. And that was at Christmas. If he had been here, he would've noticed that Sandy and Mo were picking on her; he had saved Sky on many occasions before. But that was when he was still working for a smaller computer company, before Microsoft had spotted him and taken him over to the USA. If he had been here, Sky would not have yelled, 'Would you two idiots shut up! For once in your short, miserable lives!' and she would not be sat in her bedroom, grounded for the night. Sky sighed. She hated her bedroom. It looked like it belonged to someone in Reception for goodness sake. Her walls were pink, her bed was white and the main theme was lovehearts. *Lovehearts*. It was a wonder there wasn't a poster of Peppa Pig plastered above her bed. She had wanted it repainted blue but her sister had asked first so Sky was on the waiting list. Only Sandy had had her room painted the colour of her lipstick two months before. Oh, why did she have to be in the blasted Calling family? Nothing ever went right for her here.

Sky got up and walked over to her windowsill. On it, were the storm cloud earrings she had gotten for her birthday. They had miniature whirlwinds hanging from the bottom. Wind. Sky liked the wind and she was pretty sure the wind liked her. Back when her dad still lived with them, they had gone out for a walk; Mo on his Paw Patrol bike, Sandy in her black high heels and Sky brushing her gloves against the trees. Her mother had said, 'Ooh God, I wish the wind wasn't so blooming cold.' and then pulled her hood over her. Sky had looked over at her mum and thought *I wish it was warmer too*. And as soon as she had thought that, the wind had started blowing in the other direction with a lot more warmth. Sky had thought, *did I do that?* When she figured out that she had, in fact, changed the course of the wind (she had done this by thinking more commands) Sky had spent the remainder of the trip telling the wind what to do. And every time, it had worked. Ever since then, Sky would spend as much of her day as possible outside controlling the winds with only one question on her mind: 'Have I always been able to do this?' That question had been confirmed when Sky had put her two earrings together and seen the hologram of a pretty girl telling her that she was the element of Air and that she had inherited her powers from her father. Maybe that was why Dad liked her so much. At least this was one thing she didn't have to share. The girl had told her that there was only one of each element which was good. What wasn't good was the fact that Sky had been told to go to Tippinham Moor. Her first instinct, when she heard that, was to tell the girl, 'What? HELL NO!' And then she realised that a) the girl couldn't hear and b) she wouldn't be on her own. Apparently, the Water and Fire elements would be going too. *Great,* thought Sky. *A trio of nutters. Just what we need.*

But she felt herself flush with guilt when the girl said, 'Not only do the elements need you, the world needs you.' That had really made her feel pressured. And you should never pressure air, because you might get an explosion, which is exactly what Sky did. As soon as the hologram had finished, she flopped onto her bed and sobbed. Not too loudly though, otherwise Sandy or Mo would hear. Why did she have to go to Tippie Moor? Not only was it miles away but also, it was dangerous. People had gone missing there. Sky wasn't exactly thrilled to hear that name as her destination. But, the girl had warned her that this life was hard. She had given Sky one last chance to back out. But what life could be worse than the one she was already living? A dad who appeared to not give a fig anymore, two siblings who would be the death of her and a mum who treated two of her kids like angels and the other one like a naughty puppy that had just whizzed where it wasn't meant to. Sky couldn't live like that any longer. It was pretty obvious that her dad would not be coming back till December at the least, and if the place where the pretty girl wanted to take her was anything like a boarding school then she could always ask to come back home for Christmas, couldn't she? Sky didn't want to think anymore because her cocoa-coloured eyes were slowly shutting. She let herself drift off. Sleep now, think later. That was her cousin Tina's motto. Sleep now, think later, sleep now, think later, sleep…

*Beep, beep, beep, beep!* Good lord, Sky hated her alarm. It sounded like a demented cuckoo being strangled. She stretched and then yawned. Another normal day in the Calling household. Only it wasn't another normal day, was it? She

35

had to go to the most dangerous place she knew of, a place that everyone in Ridingthorpe was always talking about. She would be leaving her family and her home behind to follow some girl with long hair to start 'training'. Sky sighed. *That's my happy thought for the day.* She got out of bed and went over to her wardrobe. She wouldn't have any trouble packing her stuff. There wasn't enough of it. Rummaging around for her backpack and some carrier bags, Sky found some things she wasn't expecting to find. A photo of the family when Mo was little. Her Year Six 'We're All Going on a Summer Holiday' script. And her old teddy bear, Albert. There would be plenty of room for them in her bags.

Once Sky had gotten changed, packed, brushed her teeth (there was no point brushing her hair) and tied her afro back in pigtails with her favourite Scooby Doo scrunchies, she went downstairs with her bags and scoffed a pack of cheesy wotsits before anybody noticed. But it turned out that no one would've noticed her anyway because while she was halfway through stuffing a wotsits into her mouth, Sandy came downstairs in her red silk dressing gown. She walked over to the cupboard and reached for the Frosties at the back. But Sky was right next to the cereal cupboard. By now, Sandy should've made her usual snarky comment about her frizz or her scruffy trainers or the fact that she hadn't nicked any of Sandy's make-up like a normal sister. Instead, as she carried on to the fridge and pulled out the milk, Sky noticed that she also pulled out one of Mum's cocktails. Sky smiled. Now she knew why her sister sometimes acted a little weird. She would have to rat on Sandy when she got back. Sky was just about to leave when her mum's voice came from the staircase.

'Sandy? Sandy, is that you?' Sandy quickly slipped what she was holding into the pocket of her dressing gown.

'Yes, Mum.'

'Did you see that lodger Sky go out? I told her she had to leave by nine and it's ten past.' Sky's jaw dropped. A lodger? Really? She would have to have some serious words with that girl when she met her.

'No, but she's probably gone. I heard her alarm go off at eight,' said Sandy, tucking into her Frosties. Sky wondered whether she should talk to them. She didn't have any desire to be remembered as an obnoxious lodger for the rest of her life. Then, a thought occurred to her. What if her father didn't remember either? If Bruno Calling couldn't, then there was no point being here. Sky took one last look at her family and then walked out of the front door. She didn't look back.

One hour. That's how long it took the bus to get from Ridingthorpe to Tippinham. That made Sky a little cranky. Then, she found out that the only taxi going to Tippie Moor had been booked by a Fredrico Northe from 114 Oak Avenue. That made her even crankier. She wondered whether he could be her fellow element. Then she remembered that she was going to have to walk to Tippie Moor. The thought hit her like the proverbial tonne of bricks.

'Ohhh God,' she groaned, tying her scrunchie back into place. 'Can this day get any worse?' Thankfully, the man at the information desk took pity on her and told her that he would drive Sky there in person.

'Though why you would want to go to Tippinham Moor is beyond me,' said the man, chuckling. Sky hopped into the passenger seat of his Honda SUV. The plush, leather chairs were warm under her fingers.

The man leaned over from the steering wheel. 'They're heated.'

'Coool,' breathed Sky, running her nails over the seat. Her eyes came to rest on her baggy pants. She liked them because they made her look less chubby than she actually was. The man caught her staring at her feet.

'What's up, kiddo? Problem at home?' Sky couldn't say that she had been told that she was the element of Air and that she had a hard and dangerous life ahead of her. Instead, she said, 'Sort of. My dad works for Microsoft in America and he barely ever comes to see me.' Not the full truth, but not a lie either.

'Oh,' he said. He didn't pursue the matter anymore.

Ten minutes later and Sky was standing at a dilapidated shed-thing that might've once been a taxi station.

'Alright kiddo. Should I wait for you?'

'No, thanks,' said Sky, climbing out of the car. 'But thanks for bringing me.'

''S'alright. Anything for a kid,' he said and drove off. She could hear him muttering as he sped away. 'Kids,' he was saying. 'Whatever next.' That pretty much summed up the past twenty-four hours. *Whatever next.* First, you find out you have weirdo powers that are one of a kind and then you get told to wait for some random supernatural model-girl at one of the most infamous places in the south of England. Yep. Whatever next. She hefted her rucksack onto her shoulder, picked up her carrier bags and headed into the fog that lay before her.

After what seemed like a lifetime of tripping, cursing, stumbling and more cursing, Sky reached a patch of marshland that seemed a little less boggy than everywhere else. She set her bags down on the floor and sat next to them. She felt mud on the seat of her trousers.

'Oh, yuck,' she said getting up and perching on her bags instead. She wished she'd brought a watch so she could tell what time it was. Then, at least she would know how long she had been here. Thinking about it, Sky didn't even know how long it would take for her escorts to find her or if they would turn up at all. *Oh, joy,* she thought sighing. *I could be stranded here forever.* It was eerily quiet. No sound apart from the birds ahead and—wait. Suddenly, Sky heard voices on the breeze. It sounded like two people, a boy and a girl and by the sounds of things, the girl was grumbling about not wanting to be here. Then, one of them said something that caught her attention. It was the girl who had moaned, 'If we die here, who's gonna sue that weird lady?' Weird lady? Could that be the same person as her pretty girl?

The boy confirmed her thoughts by saying, 'One: we're not going to die here. And two: maybe the Air element could? They're in here somewhere, aren't they? It's not like they're going to wait forever. Or maybe they will. Who knows.' Air element? Okay, they were definitely the kids that the girl had informed her of. Sky considered shouting out and then stopped herself. That would alert anyone else in here and she really did not need that as well. The voices got closer until she could see them through the mist. They both looked about her age and the girl appeared to be flaming on her head. Sky realised it was just her hair. Oops.

'Hello?' said the boy walking over to her. Sky held her breath.

'I'm Rico,' he continued. Rico gestured towards the girl. 'And this is Gwen. What—what's your name?'

She was about to tell them. 'I' – she said and then stopped. This could be a set-up. Better to do a quick identity check first.

'Did you get a hologram with a weird lady on it?' she blurted out. Gwen smiled. Sky was instantly envious. That girl was *way* prettier than her. She seemed nice enough though.

'Yes,' she said. 'Are you the Air element?' This time, Sky smiled back.

'A 'yes' from me too,' she replied. 'And my name's Sky.'

# 5. The Carmin Woods

'Found anything useful yet?' asked Rico, looking over Sky's shoulder. She had a quick flick through the leaflet and shook her head.

'Nothing so far,' she replied. 'Was there any more at the information desk?'

'Yep. I'll be back in a sec,' he said, leaving Gwen and Sky alone. Sky looked closely at her new friend. They were perched on a bench in Tippinham's main park. It had been absolute torture on Sky's legs walking back but it had been fun. Gwen and Rico (Sky had learned they were twins – weird, huh?) were the best people Sky had ever met and the only people to accept her for who she was. They had each told their stories on the way back and Gwen had found it really cool that her dad was a rich businessman in America.

'I wish our dad was still here,' she had said glancing at Rico. 'And our mum. She could've taught you how to surf.' When Sky had asked where they were now, the twins' silence told her everything she needed to know. She felt a bit sorry for those guys. At least, they had each other now. Their own little threesome-soon-to-be-a-foursome. Only problem was, they were having a little trouble finding a way to get to their next stop: the Carmin Woods. Sky could vaguely remember hearing about them but not much. If they couldn't get there then they couldn't find the Earth element and that would be game over. And as much as Sky would've liked getting back to a sort of normal life at home, she was also interested to see who the pretty girl was. Sky didn't like to be left hanging and this was the biggest cliff-hanger that she had ever experienced. It was driving her nuts.

'Found one!' yelled Rico, as he trotted back to the girls. He handed it to Sky and then sat down on one side of her. Gwen was on the other side.

'What does it say?' she asked, peering at the tiny print.

'I'm not sure,' replied Sky, flicking through the pages. 'It says that the Carmin Woods gets its name from an evil sorceress whose cave was located in the heart of the woods. Carmin was rewarded with power by a god called Ramoth but turned bad and used her magic for evil so an enchanted warrior princess called Dragonheart had to slay her. The woods were then named the Carmin Woods after the evil witch and became forbidden territory until the 1800s when a theme park company turned it into "Carmin Forest Adventure".'

'Oh. Maybe that's what we've been missing!' said Gwen, taking the pamphlet and looking at the paragraph that Sky had been reading off. 'We've been asking for a way to get to the Carmin Woods and there isn't any. So maybe we should ask if there's a way to Carmin Forest Adventure. There's bound to be a coach stop or something for tour groups.'

'Good idea. But can one of you go to the desk this time? My legs are hurting,' said Rico.

'I'll go,' said Sky remembering something. 'If the guy at the desk is the one I'm thinking of, then we've met before.'

And with that, Sky got up and found her way to Tippinham Info, for the second time that day. She pushed open the glass door and put the leaflet on the table. 'Hi, again.'

The man looked up. It was the same man from before and he looked quite surprised at seeing Sky again.

'Oh!' he cried, dropping his newspaper. 'You again. Hello. How can I help this time?'

'I need to book a mode of transport going to Carmin Forest Adventure.'

'Alright. There are' – here he looked at his computer screen – 'two ways to get there. A taxi and a coach. Which one will it be?' Sky had a ponder. The coach would have more room, but more people. They wouldn't be able to talk freely about their mission. A taxi would be smaller but large enough for them and their bags. And the driver would probably close the connection between them and the front of the cab so they would have complete privacy. Sky made up her mind.

'Taxi, please.'

'Okay…Booked. You wanna pay now or later?' Uh oh. Sky was totally skint. Not good.

'Ummm. Just hold on,' she said turning away so she could check on her empty purse. She hoped the man wouldn't see how embarrassed she was. But when she opened it, she got a surprise.

'Oh!' she said, taking her glasses off. It was full to the brim, of twenty-pound notes. They hadn't been there before! Could it be that the pretty girl was helping them? Sky wasn't sure but she handed forty pounds over to the man at the desk.

'Now, please,' she said. 'Oh, and keep the change.' As she walked out of the door, Sky wasn't sure she'd seen anyone more startled than that man ever in her life. He looked like he'd been run over by a truck.

'Bye,' she called over her shoulder as she walked out of the door. That was one more crazy thing to add to the list of crazy things she'd done today.

'Oh great,' groaned Gwen when Sky told her they'd be taking a taxi. 'I hate those things. Don't you think a single taxi is enough for one day?' Sky wasn't sure what the story was behind that one but nevertheless, Gwen agreed to pack her bags into the boot of the cab and sit tentatively in between Rico and Sky. She looked a little green but that was all. The driver poked his head into the back.

'Where're y'all goin' today then?' he asked.

'Carmin Forest Adventure, please.'

'Okey dokey. I see y'all have already paid. That's good.' And he turned around and put his foot onto the pedal. Sky silently pushed the partition closed.

'So,' she said hesitantly. 'Any idea what we're looking for?' Gwen shook her head and Rico replied, 'None at all.'

'Oh. We'll improvise then.' said Sky looking out of the window. There were fields and hedgerows passing by so fast that she had to turn away. 'When we get there, we'll pretend to be part of a tourist group and get a map. Then, when nobody's looking, we'll sneak off.'

'You make it sound so easy,' said Rico, sighing. 'I'm still pretty confused about this whole "Elements" thing in the first place. I've not even *considered* improvising.' Gwen still didn't say anything.

'Well,' replied Sky. 'It can't be that hard, can it? All we do is find this guy and go to a ghost town. Simple. Sort of.'

Gwen looked up from the taxi's floor and said, 'Will you miss them?'

Sky looked at her and asked, 'Miss who?' even though she knew the answer.

'Your family.'

'I guess.'

'You don't sound sure.' That made Sky want to cry right there because the truth was, she wasn't sure. She loved her family because, well, they were family but none of them liked her. They all looked at her like she was devil's spawn or something. All, apart from her dad. And he had left.

'It depends really,' Sky said, staring at her feet.

'On what?'

'Well, I've told you what my family's like. It kind of depends on whether they act up or not.' Gwen got a faraway look in her eyes and then appeared to remember their conversation on the way back from Tippie Moor.

'Oh. Right. Maybe if they were nice to you then you'd miss them.'

'Yeah. That's right.'

'I miss mine.' Sky couldn't think of a reply to that one. *I'm sorry* didn't seem to cut it.

'I—yeah. Yeah.' Gwen set her head back against her seat and closed her eyes. She didn't say anything else so Sky assumed that was the end of their little chat. She wanted to say something. To make Gwen feel better. Because she did like her, she really did. But the words wouldn't come. Sky just could not imagine what it must be like. Horrible probably.

Thankfully, she was spared the awkward silence when the driver poked his head back through and said, 'Righto. We're here.' Gwen sat up. She was so enthusiastic about getting out of the car, she practically crawled over Rico. Sky climbed out and got her stuff. She waited until Gwen and Rico had collected their possessions too, and then shut the car boot.

'Thanks,' she called as the driver sped off.

'They never seem to want to hang around, do they?' said Rico, staring at the dust trail.

'No,' replied Gwen. 'It's as if they only want the money and that's all. Strange, huh?'

'Yeah, strange,' said Sky, brushing the hair out of her face. 'But I'll tell you what's even stranger.' She pointed at the entrance to the woods.

'Good Lord,' breathed Rico. 'That's just creepy.' The three of them stared at the gates. They were huge and looked like something out of a really old funfair. Sky didn't like funfairs. There were too many clowns. Gwen brushed her fingers along the rust-covered metal.

'I wonder if these are the original ones? It did say that this place was built in the nineteenth century, didn't it?' It took Sky a moment to realise that by 'it' she meant the pamphlet.

'Yeah, they might be. But that's not important,' said Rico shouldering his bags. 'We need to find this Earth dude and get out. I'm getting bad vibes just looking at it.'

'You're right,' she agreed. 'Come on then.' And so, the threesome-soon-to-be-foursome made its way into the Carmin Forest Adventure Park.

'Left.'
'Right.'
'*Left.*'
'*Right.*' Gwen and Rico were having a minor dispute on which way to go. It had taken them half an hour to get tickets

and fifteen minutes to get to the base of the zip line with the rest of their 'tour group' and they had slipped into the woods from there. They were now in the heart of the forest and Sky was pretty sure that the elemental twins were getting themselves lost.

'You have no idea where we're going, do you?' said Sky, rubbing her temples.

'Well, maybe if I had the map then I would be able to have a go at finding a route!' cried Gwen, stamping her foot. Once she had had her mini-temper, she sighed.

'I'm sorry, Rico. Carry on. I'm probably just being annoying.'

'Nah, it's fine,' he replied, but Sky could tell he was holding back a smile. 'Maybe if we wait, this guy will find *us* instead of the other way around.'

'That, my dear brother,' said Gwen, smiling back, 'is an extremely good idea. I think I may have dead legs so waiting is music to my ears.' It wasn't music to Sky's ears though. All this time, she had been *waiting* to find their final element just to stop searching? All of a sudden, something rustled above Gwen's head. She grabbed Rico's arm.

'Hate to sound like a total chicken but what was that?' she said glancing upwards. There was another rustle above Sky this time.

'There it is again,' Sky said. 'Guys get ready to run. It might be a—' But she never got to finish her sentence. Because a boy in scraggy clothes had just jumped out of a tree. He had dirty blonde hair, red eyes and a backpack was slung across his shoulder. A belt with a big rock-shaped buckle was tied around his waist and his blue shirt was crumpled and ripped.

'Hi,' he said, staring at Sky and her companions. 'Who are you?' Rico started to speak but Sky cut in.

'Did you get a hologram with a weird lady on it?' The boy glanced at his belt.

'Yeah. Who *are* you?'

'We're your escorts.' The boy considered this.

'Oh. I'm Harvey. The element of Earth.'

After a quick talk, Harvey agreed to take them to his makeshift camp. They had all voted that going to the ghost town now would be stupid. They needed to get to know each other first. Harvey had taken them on, what seemed to be a wild goose chase, but had actually ended up in a small clearing the size of a pond in the park. He had a fire set up and a sleeping bag strewn on the grass.

'Welcome to Camp Harvey,' he said, sitting down on the bag. 'Feel free to take a nap.' Sky sat down on the grass and took out a pack of wotsits that she had stolen from the kitchen back home. The other three sat down and looked at her jealously so she gave them a pack each too. Harvey shook his head.

'I don't like wotsits.' Sky thought it was impossible to dislike wotsits but she didn't complain. *More for me,* she thought. They sat in silence for a few minutes until Harvey said, 'So which is which?' Sky didn't understand but Rico did.

'I'm Rico. The Water element,' he said and then waved a hand at Gwen. 'And this is Gwen. She's Fire.' Gwen raised a hand and said 'hi' in a meek voice and then went back to her wotsits. Rico didn't say anything else so Sky introduced herself.

'I'm Sky,' she said. 'The' – Harvey didn't let her finish.

'Air element?' he completed. 'Yeah, that figures. Your name is 'Sky' and the other two aren't air which means you are.' Sky was pretty sure she could've said that on her own. This guy was kind of annoying. And she'd only known him for twenty minutes. Rico noticed that Sky was eyeing Harvey and so tried to break the awkwardness.

'So…When are we heading off?' Gwen looked like she had plucked up the courage to say something and took a deep breath but Harvey interrupted again.

'I think we stay the night here,' he said, stoking the flames on his fire. 'Going now would mean trying to find our way out.' Nobody argued but nobody looked happy. Gwen noticed Harvey attempting to keep the fire going.

'You could just ask me to help,' she said in a small voice.

'What?' asked Harvey, getting ruder by the minute. Gwen looked very irritated.

'I said, you could just ask me to help,' she said glaring at Harvey. 'Are you deaf?' Sky had a gut feeling that he knew exactly what Gwen meant. Harvey burst out laughing.

'Ooohhh, fiery temper!' he teased, grinning at Gwen. 'That would figure though, wouldn't it? You *are* fire.'

Gwen looked like she wanted to hit something. She pulled out a pile of clothes from her bag and made it so it was like a pillow.

'Goodnight,' she said, turning over. As she lay down, Sky could see there were tears in her eyes. She would not tolerate this Harvey kid if all he wanted to do was to tease her new friend.

'What was that for?' she cried, defensively. 'That was just mean.'

'Mean?' he replied. 'I was stating the truth, that's all. Now, if you don't mind, Gwen has the right idea.' And with that, he lay down on his sleeping bag and closed his eyes. Sky waited until he was snoring until she spoke to Rico.

'What a pig,' she said. 'Can't even be nice to someone who's going through the same troubles.' Rico looked back at her.

'I agree,' he said. 'That guy can't be trusted. Or if he can, he's not making it easy. He's right though. We should get some sleep. Might make us less grumpy in the morning.' And then Rico rolled over too, leaving Sky alone under the fading sunlight. She didn't see how a group of teens with a particularly irritable member were ever going to be less grumpy but she lay down and let herself drift off. Tomorrow was going to be big. Huge. They would meet the pretty girl and go with her to find out all the secrets of the elements. All the mysteries of the cosmos. And although she disliked Harvey, she was still among friends. And as long as she was with friends everything would be alright. Wouldn't it?

# 6. Harvey

Harvey did not like his home. He did not like his bedroom or his kitchen or his living room or his hallway. To be honest, nobody on the Buckstead Estate liked their house. They were all grimy, all damp, all tiny and all cheap. And Harvey could've tolerated it if his dad hadn't scarpered leaving his mum alone. His mum, Aysha, used to be bubbly and happy and they went to the beach as a family. They would dig in the sand for hours and Harvey would find so many fossils and shells in the dirt you wouldn't believe it. His mum would call him her 'little Earth Prince'. But then, Dad got a new girlfriend and left and now all Harvey's mum did was loll around on the couch watching TV all day. She neglected to clean so the house was even grosser than usual and, every day, Harvey would come home and find his mum staring at some dopey soap. So, it was up to him to make dinner. Normally, he would stop off at the local fast-food place on the way home from school; Freddie's Fries maybe or Pizza Hut if they were lucky and on the rare occasions that he forgot, he just made them beans on toast. He put his mum's food on a tray and ate his own then trudged upstairs to do nothing for a few hours. He would fall asleep, wake up, traipse up to Buckstead High, tolerate a whole day of boring Year Nine work, leave, stop off for dinner, come home and do the whole thing again. Day after day after day. No wonder Harvey was so grumpy all the time. His perfect life had turned sour just like the milk in the fridge.

It was a particularly soggy Monday when Harvey received the hologram. He had trudged home from school feeling even more miserable than usual. The bullies in Year Eleven had been picking on him. They did this anyway and Harvey could put up with it, but today they had gone too far. Like: 'Hey, Harvey. Been on holiday recently?' and 'Hey, Harvey. How's your dad? Oh wait, you don't know!' They knew perfectly well that Harvey's mum could not afford a holiday and they also knew that his dad had left. Yet, they persisted on teasing him. And he couldn't even go home and tell his mum because she would just say, 'Oh grow up' or 'Deal with it' or 'Tough doodies for you then'. So, he tolerated it for a day and then walked back home, his hood over his floppy hair. He then stumbled upstairs and lay on his bed. Harvey sighed. There was a small leak in the bathroom next door and all he could hear was *plip, plip, plip* as it fell into a bucket and the blaring of the TV downstairs. Oh, how he wished he could move out and be anywhere but here. He stared around his room. It was depressingly boring. Grey walls, a grey carpet with stains, grey bedding, grey curtains, grey hole-ridden netting that covered the window. Absolutely rubbish. In fact, if someone asked Harvey to describe his life using only one word, that word would be 'grey'. Miserably grey. He got up and shut the curtains so he could turn his lamp on. It would be lighter in his room if he did. As he walked over to the windowsill, he noticed something hanging on his tiny wardrobe. It was the cowboy belt with a rock-shaped buckle that his dad had brought back from America when he was Harvey's age. Harvey hadn't seen that thing for years. Actually, it hadn't been out of the cupboard for ages and Harvey wouldn't have just taken it out. So he picked it up but as he did so, a bright burst of black light pierced through his bland room. He dropped the belt and fell back against his bed and watched in fascination as a pretty girl appeared and explained how he was the element of Earth and how he had to go to the Carmin Woods and wait for three people. Three very specific people, actually. Harvey wasn't exactly ecstatic at the thought of meeting new people; he always managed to be rude and irritating somehow. He did, however, know the format of the woods pretty well though. A few months after his dad had left, Harvey's mum had taken him on a brief camping trip. They weren't meant to be inside the woods without a guide, but nobody spotted them. They had a whale of a time exploring and since Harvey had a photographic memory, he now knew the layout like the back of his hand.

Harvey tied the belt around his waist and lay back on his tediously grey bed. All his life, he knew that he wasn't just a loser on a sad estate with no friends. Everyone is destined to do something; they just have to find out what it is. And now, Harvey knew what he had to do, he was determined to do it right. Or as close to right as Harvey Thompson could get.

'OH! Darn!' *Smash!*

Harvey was woken up to the sound of his mother cursing and dropping things in the kitchen. Why she was in the kitchen, Harvey wasn't sure since he made breakfast every day. He grabbed a sleeping bag and shoved some clothes and rations into a rucksack, got his trainers on and trudged down the stairs. He almost made a mess of even that. There were holes where his toes were supposed to be so every time Harvey put his foot down on a step, he tripped up. He hoped there were new shoes wherever he was going.

He stumbled into the kitchen and his mum was standing in the middle of the tiny room staring at a huge eggy mess on the floor. It appeared that she had been attempting to make fried eggs but had failed miserably at the 'cracking the eggs open' stage. She was holding a 'Plenty' wet wipe in one hand and sloppy eggshell in the other.

'Oh god,' she said. 'I can't even make fried eggs.'

'Mum,' asked Harvey, stepping over the nuclear breakfast bomb, 'can I help?' Aysha didn't even blink. She just carried on looking at the eggs like they should be cleaning themselves up at this point. He stared at his mother. He yelled 'MUM!' at the top of his lungs but nothing happened. She just didn't notice him. So, he tried to get her attention another way.

'I'm running away,' he said, showing her the backpack and the sleeping bag. Nothing. Instead, she decided to mop the floor up.

'Fine,' said Harvey, choking up. 'You can just ignore me. See if I care.' He looked down at his mother's skinny frame. He used to love spending time with her. Now, he wouldn't miss her one bit. He walked out of the front door and slammed it shut.

As he ran through the streets of the Buckstead Estate, his mind was ticking. How would he get to the Carmin Woods? He had no cash. He felt in his pocket and pulled out a five-pound note. How had *that* got there? He didn't complain when he noticed it was just enough to hop on a bus and take a ride. He ran even faster as he went around the corner of Green

Lane. That was where all the bully kids lived. He saw Brian Davies and his girlfriend Britany Carla who were leaning against a signpost.

'Hey, Harvey,' yelled Britany when she saw him. 'Where are you running to? You're not scared of Brian, are you? COWARD!'

Harvey ignored their snide comments and kept on running. He eventually turned a corner that took him out of the estate and onto the main road that ran through his town. He jogged over to a bus stop and caught his breath. An old lady was sat on the other side of the bench and she tutted at him.

'Too young to run away,' she muttered under her breath. Harvey was too tired to take offence.

When the number 102 finally turned up, Harvey handed over his money and sat at the very back. Nobody sat next to him which wasn't a surprise; he was scraped all over the place from sprinting so hard. Harvey stared out of the window. He opened his rucksack and went through what he had actually packed: two shirts, a pair of joggers, a jacket and some crisps that had been stashed under his bed. *Not much to go on,* he thought. He sat there gazing at the passing trees for the next twenty minutes. The bus dropped him off with a couple of other people at a really creepy set of gates that looked like they'd been rusting for ages. Instead of following the other people to find a tour group, he casually walked off into the trees and then broke into a sprint when he thought that no one could see him.

He ran and ran and ran until he thought he saw a familiar clearing up ahead. It was the same clearing that he and his mum had camped in all those years ago. Harvey threw his sleeping bag on the floor and flattened it out. He sat down and waited. Harvey realised that it was actually quite cold and so gathered a few dry sticks from the edge of the woods and rubbed some rocks together. Soon, a small flame was flickering next to him which would make the waiting less intolerable. He waited for about half an hour and then realised that the people he was waiting for probably didn't know the woods as well as him. So, he got up and started into the forest. He explored for a while and then climbed a tree and decided that from now on he would jump from branch to branch like a little blonde monkey.

Eventually, he heard voices from below him. It sounded like two girls and a boy. He rustled the tree he was sitting in. One of the girls yelped.

'Hate to sound like a total chicken but what was that?' she asked. He rustled the tree again and the other girl said, 'There it is again. Get ready to run, it might be a—'

Harvey chose that moment to jump down from the tree. He had been pondering what to say when he met them and, in the end, decided on something short and to the point.

'Hi.'

They partially introduced themselves and then went back to Harvey's camp. He looked back occasionally and saw that the girl with the red hair (very pretty) was a little nervous, the boy was staring at him intently and the other girl with the hair like a bird's nest (not so pretty) was cursing as she tripped over tree roots. Harvey resisted the urge to laugh.

After about twenty minutes, they arrived at the clearing.

'Welcome to Camp Harvey,' he said. They were all staring at Harvey and he felt a little uncomfortable. They would already know each other a bit and Harvey didn't know a shred about any of them. So, he tried to break the ice.

'So, which is which?' he said. Not very clear but the boy seemed to get it. They then introduced themselves. Harvey noticed the fire was getting smaller and so he picked up a stick and shoved it in.

'You could just ask me,' came a voice. He looked up and saw the red-haired girl, Gwen, staring at him.

'What?'

'I said, you could just ask me!' she said. 'Are you deaf?' Harvey found it very amusing that this small ginger girl was shouting at him. He burst out laughing.

'Ooohhh, fiery temper!' he teased, even though he knew he shouldn't. 'That would figure though, wouldn't it? You *are* fire.'

Gwen looked very cross indeed about that remark. She brought out some clothes and laid them on the ground. 'Goodnight,' she said.

Sky glared at him. 'What was that for?' she cried. 'That was just mean.' Harvey was getting irritated.

'Mean?' he said. 'I was just stating the truth, that's all. Now, if you don't mind, Gwen has the right idea.' He turned over and pretended to be asleep. There was silence for a few minutes until Sky started busting out the insults. No surprise there. Even she stopped after a while and Harvey was left in silence. He would have to find a way to apologise. In the morning…

# 7. The Weird Lady
# Who's Not-Really-Weird

'WAKE UP!' For the second time in two days, Harvey was woken up to somebody screaming. He opened his eyes and saw Sky glaring at him.

'It rises,' she said looking back at Gwen and Rico.

'From the Black Lagoon,' grinned Rico to himself. Sky and the others had already finished packing their things and someone had untidily stuffed his, well, stuff into his bag. No prizes for guessing who that was. He looked over at Gwen; she still seemed a little sore about last night so Harvey decided to steer clear. Sky finished a pack of wotsits and then said, 'Come on human GPS. How do we get out of here?' Harvey was about to complain about that last comment and then thought better of it. 'Follow me,' he said, glumly.

They walked under the dappled morning light for half an hour and then emerged onto the car park near the gates. Fortunately, the only folks around were those who were staying in log cabins on-site. There were two taxis having an argument on the far side of the park. From what Harvey could hear, someone had booked a taxi and then forgotten and booked another. They were having a big row and the client just opened the door to one of them and told the other to clear off. The chosen chariot sped away while the second taxi driver cursed loudly. Sky turned around and said, 'This might be our ticket out of here.' She then jogged over to the taxi. The driver stopped yelling briefly so he could hear what Sky wanted and then nodded and climbed into the driver's seat.

'I've found us that ticket guys,' she called, looking very pleased with herself. When Gwen saw what she meant her face paled.

'Oh. My. God,' she said, rubbing her forehead. 'How many taxis does a girl have to take in two days?'

Harvey wasn't sure what that was all about, but he wanted to tell her that it would be fine, it was just a stupid taxi. But as soon as the word 'It' came out of his mouth, Gwen glared at him and said 'Save it'. She then proceeded to slam the door in Harvey's face. He sighed. He was starting to wish he hadn't been so snotty with her last night. She was a nice person and so far, Harvey's attitude was ruining what might've been a reasonable friendship. As always. He climbed in on the other side of the car and shut the door behind him. Rico was next to him, then Gwen then Sky. No surprise there. Gwen and Rico were always next to each other and Sky had decided that Gwen was now her best buddy.

As the taxi drove off, the driver asked, 'You want some music, kids?' Nobody replied but he put the radio on anyway. They sat there in awkwardness. Rico started quietly humming to himself but was quickly elbowed into silence by Gwen. He looked at her auburn hair and her enormous golden eyes. He couldn't take it anymore.

'I'm sorry about last night,' he blurted. They all stared at him as *Don't worry be happy* played in the background.

'Me?' asked Gwen. Harvey nodded.

'It's fine,' she said and then looked away. Harvey should've left it at that but he couldn't let it go.

'What do you mean, "It's fine"? Why aren't you yelling at me?' Gwen turned her head to face him.

'We were talking…We figured that you might be going through a lot. We are. Me and Rico, our parents died two years ago and we've only just got our memories back.' Harvey took a moment to process what she had just said.

'Wait…Your parents? As in both of you?'

'We're twins.'

'Oh. And yeah…you're right.'

'And Sky,' she carried on, 'her dad works in America and her siblings are brats.' Harvey smiled, weakly.

'Believe me, I know about dad problems…' He found himself telling them everything. His life, his school, his home. It all came flooding out.

'So…You forgive me?' he asked when he was done.

'Yep. Well, I do. Not sure about Sky.' Sky was scowling at Harvey but she burst into a grin.

'Course! We can talk about how we both hate our dads,' she said reaching over and flicking Harvey's ear.

'Thanks guys,' he muttered and brushed the hair out of his eyes. They spent the rest of the journey telling life stories and spilling facts. Harvey found out he was the oldest; even though they were all thirteen, Harvey was in Year Nine and the others were only in Year Eight. He also found out that he had heard of Gwen and Rico's parents.

'They were on the news when…You know.'

'Yeah…They're probably like mini celebrities,' said Rico, lightening the situation. It was quiet for a few moments but then Sky jumped.

'I know this song!' she said and started singing loudly. Harvey smiled. He'd never had friends before. It felt good. They all started singing then but were interrupted by the driver who poked his head through and said, 'We're here.' Apparently, Sky had already told him about their next destination. The abandoned mining town, Kilchester.

Kilchester did not look like the kind of place you saw in the south of England. A cowboy film set in Texas, maybe, but not East Anglia. It had once been a very productive coal-mining town but an accident a few hundred years ago had caused it to become a ghost town. However, it seemed like something else had happened to it as well. The wooden shutters of all the low, cabin-style houses were bolted shut and the doors were sealed. The elemental foursome climbed out of the car. Sky handed him two twenty pound notes. 'Keep the change,' she said. The driver didn't wait. He snatched the cash and drove away. Harvey stared at his new friends. They stared back at him.

'What now?' asked Gwen. She was happier with Harvey now and wasn't giving him dirty looks anymore.

'I'm not sure,' he replied, looking down the barren streets. 'But we might as well explore while we're here.' Sky and Rico nodded and Gwen took a deep breath.

'Sure,' she said and set off down the deserted street. The other three followed her.

After about an hour of searching, there was still no sign of the supernatural girl who was supposedly waiting for them. They had all agreed that they were looking for a two-metre-tall girl with long black hair and a white dress. No traces whatsoever. Someone like that couldn't just disappear, could they? Turns out they could. They were traipsing miserably down the main high-street. An old flyer flapped into Harvey's face: Kilchester Festival – 1 August 1894, it said. He flapped it away and joined his friends next to a main, raised section in the centre of the street.

'This is hopeless,' he sighed. 'We're never going to—' Just at that moment, a black ball of energy appeared on the raised dais. Sky, Gwen, Harvey and Rico scrambled backwards and watched in fascinated awe as the plasma ball got bigger and bigger. Suddenly, it vanished in a burst of purple light and in its place stood the most beautiful girl that Harvey had ever seen.

'It's the weird lady,' breathed Rico.

'But she's not really weird,' whispered Gwen. They were right. The girl was indeed two metres tall with a torrent of jet-black hair that flowed over her shoulders. A piercing silver streak cut down one side. She was donning a headpiece with two crescent moons attached; one pure black and one a bright white. She wore a dress the colour of snow and her skin was just as pale. The bottom of the dress seemed to spill off her like ink and her pretty feet were bare. Harvey was awestruck anyway but then she opened her eyes. Oh god. Her eyes. From a distance they seemed as black as the night itself and Harvey noticed that they were flecked with browns and purples and whites. He looked closer and saw that her eyes were like space; the colours were the galaxies. He realised with a start that the girl might've actually seen those images. She only looked about sixteen but Harvey thought she was probably way older than that. She regarded them all with those strange eyes and it seemed as if she was angry. Then she smiled and said, 'Greetings, my fellow elements.' Harvey recognised her voice from the hologram. She continued. 'My name is

Andromeda, element of Darkness, Guardian of Night, only being to be older than the dawn of time itself. I am very pleased to meet you all.' She spoke in a pleasing accent that sounded vaguely American, though it might've been something else. Andromeda held out her hand. Nobody took it. They were all too shocked to move.

'Worth a try,' she said, taking her arm back. 'Now, it would be very useful for me if you introduced yourselves. I know your parents but not you and it is vital that I know each element personally seeing as I am the head of activities.' Gwen opened her mouth to say something and then shut it again so Rico spoke for her.

'I'm Rico,' he said, lacing his fingers nervously. 'And this is my sister Gwen. We're Water and Fire.' Andromeda looked at them with interest.

'Yeees…' she said, 'I have heard of you from your parents. I will explain more about them and their deaths later. It is important that you know the reasons.'

'Reasons?' cried Rico. 'There's no reason for dying!'

'I wish that were true, Rico,' said Andromeda with sympathy. 'Alas, the Prophecy Stone doesn't think that. But enough. What about you two?' Here she gestured to Harvey and Sky.

'I'm Sky,' said Sky, frantically trying to make her hair look a little less untidy. 'Element of Air.'

'Ah, yes, Bruno's daughter,' said Andromeda, smiling. 'I was always fond of him.'

'Which means you are Earth,' she carried on, pointing at Harvey. 'I remember your mother. She always said she wanted a boy called Harvey. So, I'm assuming that's you?'

'Yup,' he gulped.

'Good,' said Andromeda. 'That means we can get going. Even for an eternal being like me, this place still gives me the creeps.' She stuck her slim arm up in the air and a wall of darkness shot out of her hand. It appeared to be sucking all the light out of Kilchester; the place was suddenly awash with gloom. An eerie thrumming sound filled the air. Andromeda's hair was flying all around her and she squinted to see what was going on inside the darkness. All of a sudden, the gloom disappeared and a sleek black hover-ship swirled into existence. All four children's jaws hit the floor. Andromeda found this funny.

'*Shadow 5,*' she laughed as a section of sleek obsidian metal slid back, revealing a door. 'The most modern way of transporting the new elements to the Mansion of Night. Way ahead of its time; bad boys like this aren't scheduled to be invented till the 2090s.' A face popped out of the doorway. It was a young boy, about fourteen years old with floppy brown hair, a mischievous grin and a black cape around his shoulders.

'Wonderful morning, m'lady,' he said, shielding his eyes from the glare of the sun.

'Get back into the cockpit, Twiz,' said Andromeda, rolling her eyes. 'And try to remember your training. Please.'

'Sure thing, m'lady,' he grinned and hopped back into the *Shadow 5*.

'Don't mind him,' said Andromeda, bending down as she climbed through the opening. 'He's been with me for thirty-one-years and he still hasn't grown up one bit.' She let that sink in.

'Thirty-one-years?' asked Harvey. 'But he only looks—'

'He only looks about fourteen, yes I know,' completed Andromeda. 'He was lucky. Most of my assistants don't lose any years when they join me but some do. Twiz here was seventeen when he pledged his loyalty. It was 1989 and well…'

'I was a pizza deliverer and I got the wrong address,' came a voice from inside *Shadow 5*. 'As soon as you join, you become immortal. Andy will explain more when we get back.'

'Don't call me Andy!' cried Andromeda. She sighed. 'He's right though. We really should be going now. You start your training at six.' She climbed through the doorway which didn't leave them much choice but to follow her. Harvey went in first, then Sky, then Gwen and Rico. And what he saw inside completely blew him away.

On the outside, *Shadow 5* looked about the size of a large family car. On the inside, it was at least three times as big. There were two rows of black metal benches which were lined with leather. The ceiling was striped with beams and on them were plastic handles like at the top of a bus. A circle of light glowed from the far side of the hovercraft. Harvey guessed that was the cockpit. Andromeda was holding onto a beam and grinning.

'Welcome to my hover-ship,' she said. 'I hope you like it.' Harvey nodded and sat down on a bench next to Sky.

'Alright, Twiz, we're ready to go!' she yelled. 'Don't crash!'

'I'll try not to!' Twiz called back and started the engines. That didn't exactly reassure Harvey. Andromeda grinned even more. 'This whole machine is coated with eco-friendly solar panels,' she said. 'It's also invisible to the mortal eye so you don't have to worry about being spotted.' She surveyed the four children in front of her. Harvey couldn't help but notice that Andromeda's smile looked slightly pained. Like she was hiding something. Or maybe she wasn't as open as she appeared to be. She could have all sorts of things going on; she did say she was 'head of activities' whatever that was. Harvey wasn't sure but his train of thought got broken anyway.

'So,' said Andromeda. 'Do any of you have any questions before we get back? My partner won't be interested in listening, just talking.' Rico put his hand up.

'Yes,' he said, slowly, 'You said that there was a reason that our parents died. What's that all about?' Andromeda shifted uncomfortably like this had already turned into a touchy subject.

'Well…I mentioned the Prophecy Stone, didn't I? It's a huge block of swirling solidity that was created when the elements first took on the forms of humans. If it puts its mind to it, it would be even more powerful than me. See—' Andromeda paused. 'It has what you would call a super-elemental force. That kind of stuff can wipe out entire continents. When the Prophecy Stone was created, it knew that it was strongest. It thought that it ruled the roost. And so,' she said, 'it gave us rules that the elements have to follow. And if you break those rules, there must be a forfeit.' Andromeda looked like she was close to tears. 'One of those rules was that elements cannot fall in love and have children. Because if they pass down their powers, there might only be one element. There might be two of the same. It had never happened before so we didn't actually know. And so, when you were born, we were just so relieved that there was one of

66

each. But your parents still broke the rules. And the Prophecy Stone never forgot that.' Andromeda knuckled her eyes.

'And the forfeit was the car crash,' said Rico, staring straight ahead.

'I'm sorry, Rico. And you too, Gwen. But what is done cannot be undone.' She took a deep breath and then suddenly the whole hovercraft lurched forward. Andromeda seemed to know what the problem was immediately. 'TWIZ!' she yelled, rubbing her head which she had hit on one of the beams. 'I thought I told you to remember your training!'

'But I don't want to!' cried Twiz. 'It brings back bad memories!'

'Yes, but it might just save the lives of the FOUR MORTALS we have with us!' she yelled back. 'You might be immortal, but they're not!' Harvey clung to his seat.

'What does he mean, it brings back bad memories?'

'Well…' said Andromeda. 'I might have been a little *too* generous when I passed him on the test that would let him drive this thing. The only thing he could drive in the eighties was…'

'Was what?' asked Sky.

'A moped,' said Andromeda, miserably. 'Every other thing that he's driven he's either crashed or broken. Sometimes both.'

'Then why did you pass him on the test?' queried Gwen.

'Because no one else was willing to drive it,' said Andromeda. 'Hovercrafts are extremely useful when they work but sixty-seven-point three percent of the time they are actually quite dangerous. It won't harm the driver, obviously, because they can't die but it is still pretty petrifying to be stuck in a flaming two-tonne hovercraft that is plunging towards the ground at two hundred miles per hour.' Harvey gulped. That particular fact did not bode well because they were currently sitting in one of those extremely useful but dangerous two-tonne hovercrafts right now.

'Anyhow,' said Andromeda, rubbing her eyes. 'We're almost there now so as long as Twiz doesn't crash us in the next six hundred metres' – here she glared in the direction of the cockpit, – 'then we should be fine. Should.' Harvey gulped again. After a few seconds, Andromeda smirked and said, 'Hold onto your hats ladies and gentlemen. Hovercraft landings aren't always the smoothest.' Harvey braced himself but he had to hand it to Twiz – he did a pretty darn good job of landing *Shadow 5*. It was similar to being in a landing airplane; not the 'hang onto your seat, I'm going to be sick' kind, but the same feeling of gravity attempting to pull you down. He heard a beep from the cockpit and a sniffle that Harvey assumed was Twiz.

'I'm sorry, m'lady,' he said looking very sheepish. 'I tried my best.'

'Shut up, Twiz,' said Andromeda scowling. 'Not everyone wants to hear your grovelling.' But then her expression softened and she said, 'I know you tried your best, Twiz. I appreciate that.' Twiz looked like his whole week had just been made. The doorway in the side of the hovercraft slid open and Andromeda hopped out. 'Come on, you four,' she said, smiling. 'I think it's about time you saw my mansion.' Harvey climbed out and almost had a stroke. What a mansion it was! It was about the size of a stately home but instead of being made of brick or stone, the entire building was made out of a shiny black material. It looked very out of place in the sunlight, but not ugly. In fact, it was the most elegant building

Harvey had ever seen. There were two towers looming above the entrance and the occasional window glistened purple in the light. A set of huge wooden doors were standing at the base of the wall. Andromeda walked over to them. Twiz, Harvey, Sky, Gwen and Rico followed her.

'Welcome,' she said, her voice filled with delight, 'to the Mansion of Night.' And she pushed open the doors.

Imagine the inside of a gigantic hall that is used for concerts and massive gatherings. Now triple it. Quadruple it, even. That is what Harvey was seeing. The inside of the mansion was coated with the same dark material as the outside only they stood on a stone walkway looking down onto a second floor below them. A vast vaulted ceiling rose above them.

'This is my place of residence, and now it is yours too until you are sixteen,' said Andromeda, walking over the bridge. 'Over there' – she gestured to the bottom right, – 'are my assistants' quarters. Above that are my own quarters which, on no account are you to go into. Down there' – here she pointed a finger to their bottom left, – 'are the engineering laboratories and test rooms. Don't go in there either. Straight ahead is where you'll live, and I'll show you that soon but first' – Andromeda paused for dramatic effect – 'first, we must meet my partner.'

'Is that the same partner who wanted us separated?' asked Gwen.

'Mmmhmm,' said Andromeda. 'He is very pleased with himself but he's alright really. Follow me.' She had crossed the walkway and was heading towards her left. A smaller pair of wooden doors stood in the centre of the wall.

'What's through there?' asked Sky.

'Through there is what I like to call the Suspended Connection. It links my residence to my partner's.' Andromeda pushed open the doors and revealed a long corridor that was lined with stained-glass images. Through the occasional section of transparent glass, Harvey could see that they were really high up.

'Come on,' said Andromeda, walking towards a final pair of doors. 'He doesn't like latecomers.' When everybody else had caught up, Andromeda turned around and whispered, 'Welcome to the Palace of Day.' And once again, she pushed open the doors. Once again, Harvey's breath was taken away by truly magnificent architecture.

# 8. Flare and Andromeda

'Whoa,' breathed Rico when they walked in. 'This place is epic.' It was a mirror image to the Mansion of Night, only this time, they were on the bottom floor.

'My partner always liked to think of himself as higher up than me,' sniffed Andromeda. 'Even though I am actually superior, whether he likes it or not. This place is exactly the same set-up as my place, only there are no Elemental Quarters and way more laboratory space.' She headed for a grand central staircase that curled up towards the second floor. She then made her way to yet another doorway that was in the same place as the one that led to the Suspended Connection in the Mansion of Night. Andromeda turned to face them. 'Now,' she whispered. 'My partner can be a little full on but try not to take it personally. Also, never tell him that he's not actually busy. He may dissolve you.' Rico gulped as Andromeda knocked on the large set of doors.

A voice said, 'I'm busy!' but Andromeda opened the door anyway. She stood to one side and let the children survey the room.

'He really *is* OTT,' chuckled Twiz as he went to stand next to Andromeda. They were standing in one of the largest control rooms that had ever been constructed. Everywhere

71

Rico looked, there were a myriad of buttons and screens. People stood at desks and computers everywhere.

In the centre of the room, staring at a particularly large screen was a man. 'Ahem,' said Andromeda. The man turned around. He was the same size as Andromeda but the similarities ended there. He had skin as dark as onyx oak and he wore a three-piece suit: red blazer, orange trousers and a yellow tie. His whole body seemed to glow with a golden aura.

'Ahhh,' he said, beaming. 'The slow coaches finally arrived. Welcome to the Palace of Day. I am Flare, element of Light, Guardian of Day—'

'Eternal show-off,' said Andromeda, batting her eyes innocently. Flare stopped mid-lecture.

'You're calling *me* a show-off?' he said, frowning.

'Yep.'

'Really? Oh, that's just typical…'

'Well, if you're not a show-off, then you're an accident-prone show-off,' said Andromeda folding her arms.

'What? I don't—'

'The time you blinded those astronauts.'

'That was an acci—oh. Umm—'

'The time you burnt those crops in the Sahara starving an entire tribe to death.'

'Ahhh…'

'And the time in WW2 when you rose the sun too early making sure those fighter pilots could see the city they wanted to bomb.'

'That wasn't my fault!' yelped Flare. 'And if it was…Well, if it was, it was just a joke!'

'A joke?' said Andromeda, scowling at him. 'A whole city and half its residents crumbled to ashes? Yeah. Real funny joke, Flare.' She turned to the others. Twiz was trying his best not to laugh. 'I'm sorry, you don't want to hear us arguing,' Andromeda said. 'Flare, once you've done talking, could you get Lauren to show these guys around?'

'Sure,' grumbled Flare.

'Hey, why can't I do it?' asked Twiz.

'You've done enough today, Twiz,' said Andromeda, smiling at him. 'Meanwhile, I will be in the training hall, which you will be shown to later, setting up, drifting around, doing the same immortal-y things that I have been doing for the past few aeons.' And with that, she left the room with a flourish and a flick of her hair. Rico noticed that she looked…What was the word? Unhappy? No. Depressed? No. Lonely was the word he was searching for. She looked lonely.

'Sorry about her,' said Flare, suddenly forgetting his argument with Andromeda. 'She can be a real grumpy-pants sometimes.'

'Rude!' cried Twiz.

'You can go as well,' said Flare, pointedly. 'I don't need any of you darklings in my Palace. Lauren knows the way.'

'But—'

'Go away.'

'Okay,' murmured Twiz and he sloped off after Andromeda.

'Anyway!' said Flare, happily adjusting his golden tie. 'You came to the right dude if you want the best of the best. Biggle!' he yelled at a man in a white lab coat who was fiddling with some wires. Biggle jumped to attention. 'Yes, sir?' he said.

'Bring up the 3D virtual tour, please!'

'Of course, sir! Right away!' Flare looked at his new acquaintances.

'Put these on,' he said, handing them each a set of goggles; the kind that you got if you bought a virtual reality headset. Instantly, a flood of images burned into Rico's eyes.

'Sorry,' said Flare in a tone that made it quite obvious that he wasn't really sorry. 'Technical difficulties.' The images calmed down and Rico saw the Mansion of Night. No, not the Mansion of Night, the Palace of Day, this time from the front, not the Suspended Connection.

A voice said, 'Welcome to the Palace of Day. We will start the virtual tour in ten seconds.'

Flare made an excited sound. 'I love these things!' he said.

'Five seconds' beeped the headset. 'Three, two, on—' It didn't finish. Because the power had just cut out.

'Darn it!' yelled Flare. The entire team of electricians stared in curiosity at the blank screens.

'That's the only problem with having a whole room full of electrical items,' said Biggle, sadly. 'One goes, they all go…'

'So does that mean we can't do the tour?' said Harvey. 'I was rather looking forward to it.' Rico had been looking forward to it too. He'd never used a VR headset before.

'Sorry, guys,' said Flare in a tone that made him actually sound sorry. 'I guess that's it. Never mind. I'll call Lauren and get her to take you over to your quarters. It's six in a while anyway.' Rico stared at his watch. It was ten minutes to five. How had the day gone so quickly? It seemed like only moments ago he was staring at Andromeda's scarily beautiful eyes for the first time. Flare opened the door to the control room.

'LAUREN!' he yelled. 'YOU'RE NEEDED!' As if by magic, a girl appeared next to the door. She had long golden hair and warm green eyes.

'You called, my Lord?' she said. She had a pleasing British accent.

'Yes,' replied Flare. 'I need you to take these guys to their quarters. And show them how to get to the training hall.'

'Of course, my Lord,' she nodded. 'Come along.'

As they followed Lauren out of the door, Flare called, 'I'll show you that tour later! Bye!' And then the door shut.

'So how did you get here?' asked Harvey, as they made their way across the walkway in the Mansion of Night.

Lauren looked over her shoulder. 'Did Andromeda tell you about her assistants, then?'

'Yes,' said Harvey. 'She said, once you join, you're immortal.'

'Is that all?'

'Yep.'

Lauren sighed. 'She didn't tell you all of it then. See, the only way Andromeda and Flare can gain assistants are accidental sightings. They aren't allowed to tell regular mortals about the secrets of the Elements; it's one of the Prophecy Stone's rules. If a mortal sees them without the element knowing, that is called an accidental sighting, it wasn't the element's fault. The element can then tell them everything and the person can either choose to join the element as an assistant, if it is Flare or Andromeda, or go into the world again as a crazy.' Lauren rubbed her forehead. 'Me, I was a pilot who delivered supplies to the front lines in WW2.

75

I was twenty-five when I crashed into the Palace of Day in 1941 but I've lost some years. I feel seventeen.' Sky gasped.

'So that means you're—' she started.

'Technically one hundred and four years old, yes,' she said. 'So I can't resign my loyalty now, otherwise I'd turn into the old lady that I would've grown up to be.' Lauren shrugged. 'Enough of that. Let me show you the Hall of The Elements.'

The Hall of The Elements was the one place that Andromeda hadn't pointed out before. It was a stone doorway just like the others but it led to a long corridor that went on seemingly forever.

'It has a portrait of every single human who has ever hosted an elemental power of some sort. It started in the Bronze Age and has been growing magically ever since,' said Lauren. They wandered to the end of the hallway. There were four spaces that were large enough to fit four portraits. But something was up. Rico remembered when he and Gwen had seen the hologram back at the other house. Andromeda had said that there were actually five elements aside from herself and her partner. There were only four of them. He recalled that the missing one was Ice.

'Lauren,' he said. 'Do you know anything about the current Ice element?' Lauren stopped dead in her tracks.

'I'm afraid so,' she said and pointed at the latest portrait. 'Finneas Lebowski. I remember him quite clearly.' The portrait showed a boy with mouse brown hair that flopped over his right eye and a mad glint in the eye that you could see.

'All the elements are retrieved when they are thirteen,' said Lauren. 'We found Finneas four years ago. You have to understand…The thing about Ice is…it's not always good.'

'What do you mean by that?' Rico asked.

'Ice has two sides. The elegant-icicles-and-fluffy-snow side and the avalanches-and-smothering-farm-animals-under-piles-of-snow side. And Finneas…He was evil.

'Most of the time, 'evil' will mean that they don't like us. They just can't tolerate us. And we can put up with that. But Finneas went too far. He hated us with a passion. He stayed with us for two years until he was fifteen, and if he had stayed a little longer, he could've left when he was sixteen. But no. Finneas did something that no element has done before…'

'What did he do?' whispered Gwen, in fascinated horror.

'He rebelled. And then…Then he ran away.'

'Where is he now?' asked Sky.

'No one knows.' said Lauren forlornly. 'He's out there somewhere right now. Plotting and planning. And he's going to strike back. There's no doubt about it. The little whatsit could be in this building right now and we wouldn't have a clue. Which is why,' said Lauren pushing open the doors at the end of the corridor. 'We need to be prepared. Welcome to the Elemental Quarters.'

There were seven doors in the Elemental Quarters. Lauren explained that each was labelled for a specific person. 'The door down that end' – she pointed to the left, – 'leads to the training hall. Andromeda wants you there at six. And the one at that end' – she gestured right, – 'leads to the roof. I will give you some free advice now; never go to the roof at night. You may just find Andromeda up there conversing with the darkness and she's self-conscious when it comes to that kind of stuff.'

'What do you mean by that?' asked Harvey.

'Never mind,' said Lauren. 'Your doors are all there and…Well, I'll see you around.' And she gave one last wave only to disappear down the Hall of The Elements.

Rico stared at the door labelled 'Water'.

'Ummm…I'll see you at six,' he said. They all said their temporary goodbyes and then locked themselves in their quarters. Rico let out a breath that he didn't even realise he had been holding. He turned around. And almost fainted dead away. He had expected his "quarters" to be a poxy little room with a bed and oven and a miniscule little en suite. But it was like a whole apartment. A luxury one at that. He was standing in a kitchen/dining room and to his right was a living room. He strolled in and saw that a door led off into a bedroom that did have an en suite with a shower, bath, toilet, sink and a leather couch just in case you wanted to take a nap while you dried yourself. Rico wandered back to the kitchen area and to his left was a large room. Rico frowned and walked in. And almost cried. Because it was a study with all his things already in it. He hadn't realised, but when he had boarded *Shadow 5* his things disappeared. And here they all were with a bunch of other items he must've left at his parents' house. His mum's surfing wetsuit was hung up in a corner. The photo of him and Gwen and Mum and Dad at the beach was perched on a shelf. He couldn't help smiling at that. They were only about six at that point. Gwen's hair was plastered down her back and one of her front teeth was missing. Rico and his dad were wearing matching swimming trunks. Rico picked it up from the shelf and pressed it to his chest. He decided that that photo would be living next to his bed.

Once he had gone around the study one more time and reminisced about every object, Rico went into the kitchen and made himself a coffee. Strange as it sounded, coffee calmed him down. The clock said it was quarter past five. He had about half an hour to himself before he headed down to the training hall. His heart started beating faster all over again at the thought. He had no ideas what sort of 'training' he would be doing but considering the strange day he had had, it could be anything. He watched as a bird of prey swooped outside the window. It lunged and swerved, glided and dived. He wouldn't mind being a bird. Freedom would call around every corner. Rico looked up as the clock chimed quarter to six. He put his coffee next to the microwave in the kitchen. He would have to warm that up later. He went and put on a different pair of clothes – a white, long-sleeved T-shirt with the words "ELEMENT: WATER" printed on the back and a note saying " 'This is your new uniform, hope you like it!' Andromeda X", had been left on his bed. He pulled the shirt over his head and walked over to his "front door".

This. Was. Only. The. Beginning.

# 9. Training

Gwen wasn't sure she wanted to leave her new quarters. She absolutely loved it. It was like having her own little flat. And the study was chock-full of old memories. She had been drifting around, staring at each one intently, listening to Sky next-door saying, 'I carried all that stuff *all* that way, just to have it be here anyway! Arrgh! Why do I bother?' Gwen had chuckled at that and then went to sit on her couch in the living room. She was thinking about training. She was partly excited and partly nervous. Really nervous. Because Andromeda hadn't even hinted what they would be doing. Neither had Flare. Neither had Lauren. Neither had Twiz. Gwen and the others were totally in the dark.

She had put on some new clothes after finding a white, long-sleeved T-shirt on her bed with the words "ELEMENT: FIRE" printed on the back and a note saying, "'This is your new uniform, hope you like it!' Andromeda X", next to it. She liked Andromeda. She wasn't sure what the matter was with her, but she looked sad. And Gwen didn't like not talking to sad people. She wanted to cheer them up. So, she had decided that as soon as this 'training' was over, she would ask Andromeda what the matter was. It had to be worth a shot. The clock pinged quarter to six and Gwen scurried to the door and down the corridor. Another thing she didn't like – being late. Unfortunately, she was more nervous than she realised and spent five minutes plucking up the courage to open the door so when she did get to the stairs that led down to the training hall, and when she did tiptoe off the last step and brace herself, everyone was already there. And they all looked a lot more at ease than they had done two days ago. Sky had her hair down (or up as Sky's hair had no sense of gravity whatsoever) and her blue glasses were perched on the end of her button-nose. Harvey had his dad's belt on and was trying and failing to slick his hair back. Rico was eyeing Andromeda but when he saw Gwen, he waved her over. And Andromeda…She hadn't really changed. Her long black hair cascaded over her shoulders, her silk dress was still rippling like ink and her face was as anxious as ever. Whatever happened, Gwen was determined that she would at least try to help her.

'Hey, Gwen!' called Rico, as he jogged over to her. That was the same thing that he had said on the day they'd received the hologram.

'Hi,' she said, smiling. 'You like your quarters, sorry, luxury apartment?' Rico grinned.

'I sure do,' he said. 'You?'

'Do I like it?' she said sarcastically. 'It has all of my old things in it. I could spend hours remembering…Of course I like it!' Andromeda had noticed that Gwen had arrived. She put on her best brave face and cleared her throat.

'Ahem. Thanks for coming, all on time,' she said. 'Well. Nearly, all on time. But that doesn't matter because we're all here now. Do you like your quarters?' A chorus of 'Yes' and 'It's amazing' and 'I wish you'd told me all my stuff would be there, but yeah' filled the room, echoing up towards the vast ceiling. Andromeda gazed at Sky and frowned but then went back to her speech.

'That's good. Before we start, I just want to let you know that by the end of the day, you need to all have signed this piece of paper,' she said, wafting a small sheet in the air. 'It would be preferable if you didn't do it now because then we would be delayed and I know a few people who don't like being late.' Gwen heard her mutter 'Flare' under her breath. Those two weren't exactly soulmates. Gwen could understand. Putting up with Flare, the control freak, for trillions of years could really do something to a person.

'So,' Andromeda said. 'Unless any of you have any reason to delay the training anymore, I'll begin. Anyone?' No one put their hands up. 'Good. Then let me start.'

Andromeda took a deep breath. 'Do you see those eight doors over there?' She pointed to her left. The children nodded. 'There are two doors for each of you. An entry and an exit. There are five stages to your training that must be completed for you to pass. If it was up to me, I'd give you your first day off but it's not up to me. So, you all need to pass today or…Well, I'm not sure what happens. But the Prophecy Stone is cruel so don't chance it.' Sky looked at Andromeda.

'What exactly *are* the stages?' she said, taking her glasses off and wiping them with her shirt.

'Well, first of all they're magical,' said Andromeda. 'So, they might not be what you expect. There is a stage for each sphere of power that we have control over. If and when you pass, you can move onto the seven-stage training but for now it's just five. You can be guaranteed that you'll get through one of the stages but for the rest, your powers will be required.'

'What if we haven't used our powers yet?' asked Harvey. Just like him. Always blunt and to the point.

'You can use the time before you enter to practice a bit.'

'Cool!' grinned Harvey. 'So, what, I can just summon a big chunk of rock and lob it at you?'

Andromeda grimaced. 'I would advise against it,' she said. 'But yes, you could do that. Anything that is linked to your sphere of power, any action, and you can make it happen.' Harvey closed his eyes and the ground rumbled.

'Not now!' yelled Andromeda, stepping forward and waving her arms.

Harvey opened his eyes and smiled. 'Whoops.'

'Yes, whoops,' said Andromeda, wincing. 'You can do that once I've finished. Back to training. As soon as you step into the chamber you're stuck unless you manage to make it out to the next stage or if you yell, "Finished." Then the next door you come to will lead you out. Brains are required, people. You have to be tactical as well as powerful. I'll be here if you need me. Good luck.' And as she stood aside, the doors whirred open. A salty smell wafted out of each door, a smell that could only belong to one thing…

'The sea!' cried Rico. 'Yes! I'm first!' Gwen had no idea how an entire ocean could fit inside a chamber but Andromeda had said that it was magic. She was reluctant to go in without first trying her powers. She hadn't summoned one little fireball yet and she was unprepared. Gwen watched as her friends slowly made their way to the doors. Just to be sure, she thought in her mind, *fire, please come now. Confirm that I am who I am*. And she felt a slight tingling at the tips of her fingers; turning into a bearable burning feeling. She felt it build up until she realised that her friends might not be able to survive a bonfire. Swiftly, she aimed her hand at the nearest wall to her, just in time too. An intense burst of flame shot out of her slim fingers and turned the wall into a charred blackened mess. Gwen hadn't noticed that Andromeda was quite that close to her heat. She stood with a panicked expression on her face and her arms above her head.

'Oh! I'm so sorry, Andromeda!' yelled Gwen.

'Was that meant to scare me?' Andromeda said quietly. 'Or were you trying to kill me?'

'Neither!' cried Gwen. 'I just…'

'It's fine,' said Andromeda, brushing a fleck of ash off her pale shoulder. 'At least we know that you're not a fake now, huh?' Gwen was confused until Andromeda smiled. 'Go on, you're gonna be last,' she said. And Gwen ran towards the door of her chamber without looking back.

She skidded to a stop on a concrete slab and turned just in time to see the doors sliding shut behind her. Gwen gulped. She was stuck. She slowly slid her feet around so she was facing her first challenge. 'Oh, dang,' she said. Four days ago, she had been curled up on her bed at Rico's old home watching the TV and living her tiny, private life. If anyone had told her that in less than a week, she'd be standing on a platform, above a swirling grey ocean, wondering how the heck she was going to make it across without drowning, she would've told them that they were just a stupid idiot who'd probably hit their head and got themselves a nasty concussion. Now, she was staring at that horrible mass of water debating whether she should yell 'Finished' or not. Gwen could imagine her friends already on the second, third, fourth challenge by now and she was stuck at number one.

'Breathe,' she said to herself. 'Think. Andromeda said that brains were required so you can't lose your head now. Just take a moment and…' And suddenly something hit her. Rico had said that his element was up first, right? Rico was water. Rico was also Gwen's brother. They had some of the same genes. Which meant…No. Surely not? Could she possibly have some sort of connection with the water? Could she control it to an extent? It was worth a try.

'Hello? Water?' she said, her voice trembling. 'Can—can you hear me? If you can, then go still.' It took a few moments but slowly and surely, the water calmed down until it was smooth as glass.

'No way,' whispered Gwen. 'It listened.' Just to check that it wasn't a fluke, she asked the water to create a whirlwind and then go still again. Sure enough, the water obeyed her commands. This could give her endless possibilities! She could ask it to float her across, create an air bubble, make a giant hand…But she chose a different option. She remembered once, last year, her Religious Studies teacher had told her the story of Moses and the Red Sea. He had called upon God to move the waves aside and create a path through the water so he and his followers could get across. Okay, maybe this wasn't quite the same concept, but what if *Gwen* could move the waves, or at least ask the waves to move themselves? That would mean that the first task would be completed. She decided to give it a shot.

'Waves? Can you do me a favour?' she called across the barren ocean. 'Can you make a path through? That's completely dry?' As if by magic, the waves slowly parted and revealed a seaweed-ridden sandy path with swirling water on either side.

'Thank you,' she cried and walked over to the edge of the platform. It was a stomach-wrenchingly long way down and a small set of steps like the ones you found at a swimming pool went to the halfway point. How would she get down? Gwen decided she'd cross that bridge when she came to it. Shakily stepping onto the first rung and holding on tight to the railings, she made her way down. As she felt her foot on the last step, her heart plummeted. She was now at that bridge she didn't want to cross.

'A little help?' she yelled, her hope falling with her heart. She wasn't expecting to be heard and was readying herself to call that she was done when a wet, cold *thing* splashed her toes. The waves had listened. Gwen jumped down into the water and saw a small whirlpool beneath her keeping her afloat. It lifted her onto the sand-path and then disappeared into the rest of the water. Gwen smiled. So, she would at least pass the first test. She wandered along the path for a while, staring at the liquid walls on either side of her. It was a bit like an aquarium only with no glass to protect her if the water rushed back into place. This was not the ideal place to be if you had claustrophobia. Eventually, Gwen made it to the end of the path. There was a ladder reaching all the way to the ocean floor this time, so she shinned up it and heaved herself onto the second platform.

'Thank you!' she shouted over the once again restless waves as the door in front of her opened with a *shhhhhunk*. Gwen sighed. One down, four to go.

Walking through the second door, Gwen realised that this stage would cause her a lot less hassle than the previous one:

it was fire. There was no platform this time, only a seething mass of dead-heat in front of her. She shuddered to think if the others had been barbecued but she couldn't dwell on that. She had to concentrate on getting through this stage ASAP. There were lots of little tiny flames that gave off little heat, mixed with huge, massive bonfires that even Gwen could feel the heat of. She tried not to be distracted by the elegant flickering pieces of ash that fluttered in the air all around her but she couldn't help it. She felt alive here. Her hair was flying around her head, looking for all the world like another fire. Her golden eyes darted around her, struggling to find an exit door. She could come back later, but now she had to pass the test. A small black dot in the distance gave off a waft of cold air. The other side. Gwen rushed towards it but stopped at the last minute. This was her sphere of control. And she had literally been in her element dashing through the smoke. She wanted to stay but she knew that her friends might have already finished by now. With one last look at the second chamber, she darted through the door.

Gwen would've died if she hadn't been on high alert. She carried on running and stopped just in time to send herself flailing on the edge of another platform that ended in nothingness. A void of cold powerful air. Instead of being dark and gloomy and a depressing place in general, it was nothing like you might expect a bottomless pit to look like. There were clouds all over the place and it was a white, light blue in colour. A constant rushing sound filled the air and Gwen's hair was flying out of control. She could see the opposite platform just in front of her; annoyingly out of reach and just too far to jump. Like Andromeda had said, she needed to use her brains for this one. And there was no ocean to help her. No water in her genes. Andromeda had said that as long as it involved their power, they could do anything. Maybe she could torch a cloud and hop on? Maybe she could turn the air currents warm and use it to fly across? Oh, who was she kidding? That was never going to happen. Gwen stood and paced the platform for a while, thinking. Imaginative. Use her brain. Anything was possible…Crazy. That was too crazy. She could never do that! But then…

Gwen took a deep breath. She felt that tingling feeling in her fingers again. A small fuzzy cloud went past her and she forced herself to move closer to the edge. It was a dizzyingly high drop. Another cloud went past her. She had to be patient. Finally, she spotted a large ball of fluff floating towards her. Her fingers felt like they wanted to explode. *Not now! Not now!* She yelled inside. As the cloud aligned with her, she let all hell break loose from her fingers. She had been hoping that the force of her fire would be enough to turn the cloud to cotton crisp and then carry on making a path to the other platform and it did. As it neared the opposite concrete, it became more solid and burned like an orange, flame road to her next destination. Gwen let out a breath she hadn't realised she'd been holding. She stumbled across her makeshift path and as she stepped to safety, it hissed and spat and fizzled into nothing and the void was filled with the *swooshhh*ing sound again. She was past halfway now. Not long left. Unless the other two challenges were extremely hard, she'd be out soon. With her luck, they'd be extremely hard.

The doors slid open to reveal a sight that Gwen had not been expecting. To her left, right and front, there were immensely tall trees forming paths that lead off in all directions. The floor was craggy and rocky and Gwen was sure that she would stumble. Because in front of her was a maze. She had never been any good at mazes. All those times her primary school visited the local corn farm, one in particular was the Maize Maze, she would get lost and someone would have to come and find her. She would sit on the floor and reassure herself that it would be okay, that someone was coming right now. But this time, no one was coming. She was on her own. Gwen could feel her stomach churning at the thought of getting lost in here. She could always be a chicken and call 'Finished' but then she would have to do it all again anyway. Andromeda had said use your brains and that strategy had worked three times. But what if she didn't mean 'think of a way to use your powers'? What if she meant something else? Would Gwen have to find her way through this horrible place on her own? She really hoped not. At least, she knew her friends would probably be alright. Harvey had told her he had a photographic memory so even if he did get a bit lost, if he came to the same bit twice, he'd know. And Rico had always been good at those mazes on the school trips. And Sky…Well, Gwen had a feeling that if she didn't get through, she would accuse the maze of being 'mean' and punch through those branches to the door. That girl was like a demon. Gwen liked Sky.

As she stepped forward and prepared herself for the long, hard hours ahead, she had a thought. Trees' leaves were brittle, right? And brittle things burned. Gwen had found that she could quite easily find her way in the fire chamber. So why couldn't she turn *this* challenge into a fire challenge? There was no "why" about it. Maybe it was a bad idea to kill all these trees. Everyone was always going on about planting more trees. Then she thought of Sky yelling at an oak to,

'Move out of my way, or I will literally blow you away' and all her worries evaporated. Gwen smiled. She could burn this place to the ground if she wanted to. So that is exactly what she did. After she had finished her training, all she would remember was the screaming. She felt her fingers tingle again and then saw a wave of heat roll off her; flame after flame after flame. She saw blinding orange lights. And the next thing she knew, she was standing next to the door with the entire forest smoking and sizzling behind her. Gwen hadn't expected to be quite this powerful. She had been expecting a weeny campfire flame not a huge, devastating forest fire. Had she really done that? She had no doubt that it had been her but that was some serious burn. She'd have to remember to keep her cool from now on, just in case she accidentally torched her friends. That would not be good. As the door opened, a breeze blew into her face. There were some snowflakes floating on the wind which confirmed her guesses of what the next and final challenge might be.

'Welcome to Ice World,' muttered Gwen as she stepped through the door.

Gwen made a note to self that next time she went from sizzling-hot to freezing-cold in less than five minutes, she'd bring chilblain cream. The icy temperature hit her like a smack in the face and she could only just stop herself from curling up on the floor to try and preserve body heat. This was the kind of ice that Lauren had been talking about – the kind of ice that made people freeze to death, the kind of ice that built up in layers and smothered farm animals, the kind of ice that isolated tiny villages, cutting them off from the outside world. The kind of ice that made Finneas Lebowski turn bad. Gwen couldn't think what the challenge could possibly be, maybe it was to just try and stay alive as long as possible until they realised that you might not live much longer and that now would be a great time to open the doors. Maybe Gwen had to warm this place up too, give it a little central heating. Maybe it was like the last challenge, some sort of disorienting Ice Maze with a blizzard stinging your eyes and a cold wind stinging your face. Then Gwen noticed something, a rather large something that she had just walked straight into. She understood what the challenge was, though how she would complete it, she wasn't sure. The something that she had walked into was an impossibly, dizzyingly, vast sheet of ice. In other words, she had walked into a glacier.

Gwen slowly craned her neck upwards to see the scarily huge glacier looming over her. 'Oh, help. Oh, please help,' she muttered. 'I am going to freeze here, where nobody knows and nobody cares and I can't do a thing.' She couldn't even shout 'Finished' because she would have to get to the next door anyway which she assumed was on the other side of this monstrosity. She couldn't melt the thing because otherwise she would drown in the tonnes of water that she had just un-frozen. Maybe she could go back the way she had come? Nope. The blizzard was too strong. She would never find her way. Gwen turned her head right – nothing. Left – nothing. Wait, there was something to her left. She walked over to it. It was a thick rope cord that led straight upward, following the face of the cliff. 'You've got to be kidding me,' moaned Gwen as she slowly came around to what she was going to have to do. 'So, I really am going to die. I'll either freeze, starve or slip and fall. Knowing me, I'll slip and fall.' Gwen rubbed her eyes. She was going to have to climb the cliff.

Gwen checked that the rope was secure around her waist for the sixth time. She was not taking any chances of falling. She *was* going to survive. She felt a shiver creeping up her spine and the cold seeping into her bones. She *was* going to survive. Probably.

'I can do this, I can do this, I *can* do this,' she muttered to herself as she grabbed onto a ledge that was just above and slid her foot onto a corresponding foothold. There was some kind of path leading up with the foot and handholds sticking out, making themselves prominent. It had obviously been designed so that you *could* climb it, it was just a case of whether you had the guts to do it or not. Gwen was pretty sure she didn't have the right kind of guts because presently her liver was twisting with fear and her stomach was crawling with butterflies. Her heart had slithered up her throat and into her mouth. Slowly but surely, she made her way up the cliff. She could hear Andromeda in her head, telling her not to look down, to keep going but of course that made Gwen want to stop and look at the view. She did and her guts did not like it. Eventually, the summit of the glacier appeared just over a small ridge, Gwen hauled herself over the edge and lay in the snow panting and gasping for breath. She shakily stood up and stumbled over to the brink, clutching the rope. The sight was magnificent. She had never been to Alaska but she had seen it on TV, it looked just like it. The landscape was rugged and harsh but strangely beautiful, just as Mother Nature (or the first element of Earth) had intended it to be. A flash above caught Gwen's attention. The aurora borealis, or a very good replica, was glittering and glimmering green and pink across the top of the chamber. This was what ice was supposed to be: mysterious and supernaturally beautiful, graceful and silent.

Gwen was smiling as she walked through the door. The cliff had been worth it. If she ever met Finneas, she would ask him why he had rejected the beauty for the malevolence. There was definitely no reason to do that.

Andromeda was waiting for her when she got out with Sky and Rico next to her. There was no sign of Harvey.

'Oh, my days!' yelled Sky as she ran over. 'You're not dead! You didn't drown, or burn, or fall, or get lost, or freeze! That's awesome!' Gwen grinned. Sky's hair was even crazier than usual with frost-covered leaves and twigs sticking out at odd angles. Her glasses were cracked and one side looked like it had been hastily sellotaped back together. Sky noticed Gwen staring. 'They're getting me some new ones.' she said. Rico breathed a sigh of relief and raced over too. He wrapped her in a bear hug which must have been difficult because they were the same height.

'I'm glad you made it,' he whispered.

'I'm glad *you* made it,' she replied. Once Rico had untangled himself, Andromeda drifted over.

'Congratulations!' she said, beaming. 'You are now a qualified element. You probably didn't notice, but there was a camera embedded in your shirt. I saw everything. What you did in stage one? That was something wicked. No one has ever been able to do that. Control something out of their sphere of power. I'll have to get you some one-to-one sessions.' Gwen could tell that Andromeda was excited. Her eyes were lit up and she glowed with a silvery aura.

'Sure,' Gwen agreed.

'You were amazing,' said Rico. 'I didn't think you'd make it past the maze. But you totally burned it. Literally and figuratively.'

'You were epic!' cried Sky. 'I'm not even sure *I* was as epic as you.'

'What did you do in the maze?' asked Gwen. Rico snorted.

'Well…I tried to get around for a bit but then I realised I was never gonna get through. So, I said, "You think…you think I'm gonna give up? Well, you are darn wrong, forest! Darn wrong!" And then I blew everything down with a mini hurricane. It was so cool.' Gwen smiled. *Demon*, she thought.

Then she remembered something. 'Where's Harvey?' Andromeda rolled her eyes.

'He chickened out at the water stage,' she sighed. 'He should be coming out soon though, unless he's frozen to death at the last stage.' As if by some sort of magic, there was a beeping sound from next to them and the exit door marked *Earth* slid open. A very bedraggled and exhausted looking Harvey stumbled out and then lay flat out on the ground.

'Thank God,' he said. 'It's over.' Sky ran over and reeled out the same lines as she had with Gwen, only she didn't yell them this time.

Rico went and helped him up, giving him a pat on the back. 'Well done,' he said. Gwen just smiled and wished she had something to say. Andromeda went on about how that was a great comeback and how it won't be as hard next time. After Harvey had recovered and wasn't so much gasping but breathing, Andromeda clicked her fingers and a small piece of paper appeared.

'Now that we're all recovered,' she said, 'I think it's time that you signed this and then got to bed. You've been in there for nearly two hours, it's eight o'clock. Once you've finished with this, just throw it into the air and it'll disappear. I want to see you all at eight o'clock tomorrow so I can explain everything in greater detail. But I think that is enough for today. I will see you then.' And she walked briskly back up the stairs with a flick of her hair.

'She seems in a better mood,' said Harvey. 'You know…More lively. Has anyone got a pen?'

'I have,' said Rico. They all signed the sheet of paper until it was just Gwen left. She took it and wrote her name so it read:

> **Water:** Rico Northe
> **Fire:** Gwendoline Northe
> **Air:** Sky Calling
> **Earth:** Harvey Thompson
> **Ice:** …
> **Darkness:** Andromeda
> **Light:** Flare

'I wonder if that guy's ever gonna come back?' said Sky peering over Gwen's shoulder as she wrote her name. 'He sounded like a right obnoxious so-and-so when Lauren told us.' Gwen pondered. Lauren had said that Finneas would come back one day, but not for good reasons. She had said that when he did come back, he would have a load of tricks up his sleeve. If he was of the same generation as Gwen and her friends, then he might come back soon. So, they would have to brace themselves.

'I don't know,' said Gwen folding up the piece of paper and throwing it into the air. It dissolved mid-chuck. 'But right now, we need z's. Like, a lot of z's. We need *sleep*. And I don't know about you, but I'm shattered. So, I'll see you guys in the morning. I have a feeling that something very big is going to happen very soon. Prepare yourselves.'

# 10. Bethany Hill

'Stupid.'

*Kick!*

'Ugly.'

*Kick!*

'Dad.' Bethany gave one last attempt to mutilate her bedframe and then gave up. She had been trying to get over what her dad had just come upstairs and told her. 'Guess what?'

Bethany had groaned. 'You're starring in the brand-new movie, *Crystal II*! And...Hollywood wants you! Isn't that awesome?'

Bethany had shaken her head. 'Ah, well. You're going anyway. Grumpy-guts. Sunday, Bethany. You have until Sunday to compose yourself, alright?' No response. Her dad had shrugged and then walked out of the room.

'Sunday!' he called over his shoulder.

'Sunday,' grumbled Bethany.

Grumbling was all she ever seemed to do these days. Ever since...Well, ever since she was six. She used to live on a farm/ranch in New Jersey with both her mother *and* her father but her mother had never wanted to go to LA or anywhere big like that. So, Bethany had been born and raised at Hill's family farm, quite happily. She had a best friend, Bobby. She had a horse, Chestnut. Best of all, she'd had her parents together. Now, she didn't have any of those things. Her parents always argued, until one day Bethany heard her father say, 'I'm going. To LA. I can't live in this place anymore. It's too…Country.' Bethany had secretly been very excited about this. Until her dad had then said that he was taking Bethany with him. At that point, she ran down the stairs yelling, which forced them out the next day. No goodbyes, no last-minute hugs. They just left. She had cried all the way to LA which was a very long time to cry for. She had cried as her father carried her and her belongings into the lift and out into their luxury penthouse suite. She had cried herself to sleep that night. She had cried all the next morning. She would've cried all afternoon too but by that point she was so exhausted; she gave up. Bethany had begged her father to take her back to New Jersey but he had only said, 'It's better for you here. You'll make quite a nice little actress, huh?' But she didn't want to be an actress. All her life, she had only wanted to be a ranch-worker, a horse rider or a survival guide in Canada.

If you asked most six-year-olds whether they wanted to be famous and rich and have designer clothes, they would have replied, 'OMG, yes!' But Bethany hadn't been asked. She'd been forced. For two years, she had put up with her snobby private school and then when she was eight, she had received her first movie offer. Bethany had turned it down but her father had said she wasn't old enough to do that. And so, she starred in her first movie, the daughter of the main character in some sci-fi/action. Afterwards, her least favourite talk show host, Moya, had asked how she felt about her father, the famous actor Manfred Hill.

Bethany had said, 'I hate him. I wanna be in New Jersey with my friends but he makes me be here! It's not fair! I hate everything.' And from that moment on she had been a total misery-guts. Hollywood thought she was a perfect child to convey grumpy teens who become action heroes or the girlfriend who involves herself in some mystery with her geeky scientific boyfriend. She was fourteen-and-a-half now and was already counting down the days till she was free of all the acting nonsense. Unfortunately, nothing could change the fact that her face was plastered all over teen boys' walls with the words 'hot stuff' scrawled all over but if she moved back to her mother then no one would see her anyway. She would disappear from the face of the Hollywood Earth. Never to be seen again.

But for now, she just had to suck it up. She was fifteen on her next birthday, so only three more years after that. Ugh. Birthdays. The worst day of her year. Her stylists would come and coo over her and dress her up like she was some 3D Barbie with the name 'Miffed Bethie'. Then she'd go out for a fancy dinner with kids she barely even knew. Even though it was supposed to be her birthday party, she would sit at the corner of the table being ignored by everyone. Yep. Worst day of her year. Actually, every day was the worst day of her year. Like it had been for almost nine years now.

'Bethany?' came the irritatingly posh voice of her personal assistant who was ironically called Butler.

'Yes, Butler?' she replied.

'Your father has a guest over for dinner and he would like you to be down by six. He also wants you to wear your yellow frock.' Bethany made a face.

'Does it *have* to be the yellow one?'

'Her favourite colour is yellow. The exact same shade that your dress is.'

'Her favourite colour is puke-yellow?' Butler sighed.

'Please, Miss Hill. Don't be uncooperative.'

'I shall be as uncooperative as I see fit.'

'But your guest is none other than the director Amelia Garcia. Your father has spoken very highly of you to her.'

'Oh, yes, Butler. We wouldn't want to upset my father's prissy little girlfriend, would we?' said Bethany, in her best imitation of Amelia Garcia. Bethany had been in a few films that had been directed by her and she was positive that Amelia hated her with a passion. Butler sighed again.

'Six, young lady. You have half an hour to get yourself ready. It won't be me in trouble.' And he stalked out of the door with his snooty, ratty little nose in the air. Bethany poofed out her cheeks and made a gagging noise. The last thing she wanted to do was spend an uncomfortable evening with two people whom she hated and one person who hated her back. She was bound to die of boredom. Then again, maybe that wasn't such a bad thing. It would certainly spare her a horrible life. Bethany decided that she would try not to die of boredom. It would all be worth it if she got to see her mother again when she was eighteen. So, she walked over to her impossibly large closet and rummaged around until she found her awful yellow dress. She was sure that Amelia's favourite colour was actually crimson and her father just wanted her to be embarrassed in the hope that she stayed quiet. Well, he was wrong. She was going to be loud and obnoxious and act like a total menace. Bethany pulled the dress over her head. It barely fitted and it was tight everywhere, some places more than others. It really was a disgusting mustardy yellow with a lace trim around the hem that went down horribly low for a girl's dress. She thought if she was going to look like a supermodel-zombie, then she may as well go the whole hog and wear heels too. She found the most outrageous wedges and slipped them onto her tiny feet. She adjusted her hem so it wasn't totally mortifying. And she walked out of the door and down to the dining room.

'Bethany! How…delightful…to see you again!' cried Amelia when Bethany walked into the room. She noticed that Amelia had forced that last sentence out like she was trying not to gag on prune juice.

'Ms Garcia,' Bethany replied. Her father made a rolling gesture with his hands like about how he wanted her to go on.

'How pleasant it is to see you too.' Bethany frowned. 'Actually, no. That's dishonest and I'm always being told to be honest, so let me rephrase Ms Garcia. How *un*pleasant it is to see you.' Amelia wrinkled her nose.

'Honestly, Manfred,' she sniffed. 'I would've thought that teaching your child manners would be high on your priorities' list. I did point that out to you last time.'

'Of course, Amelia,' smiled Manfred. 'Bethany. Sit down now. I did tell you to compose yourself.'

'I thought you told me I had until *Sunday* to compose myself.'

'I—Bethany. Just do as you're told. For once. You're almost fifteen now, sweetheart. Grow up a bit.' Bethany shrugged and sat down at the opposite side of the table to her father. She quietly slipped her shoes off under the elaborate tablecloth.

'So, Manfred…Are there menus or is it a surprise?' asked Amelia.

'Oh, there are menus,' said Bethany, batting her lashes innocently. 'But the chef is so OTT, I wouldn't be surprised if you ordered a lasagne and you received a vegetarian ratatouille with a siding of salad and garlic-stuffed dough balls.' Manfred glared at his cheeky daughter.

'Bethany, if I hear another disrespectful word come out of your mouth, you'll go straight upstairs,' he growled. *Alright, Dad, I guess I'll just carry on being disrespectful then,* thought Bethany.

'Of course, there are menus, Amelia,' said Manfred. 'Just excuse Bethany. She's a little…' he trailed off.

'A little what?' asked Bethany. 'A little cheeky? A little rat? A little she-devil? A little mean?'

'BETHANY!' cried Manfred. 'I thought I said—'

'I was being disrespectful to myself,' Bethany pointed out, calmly. 'Not to our guest.' Manfred took a deep breath.

'Just order your food, please,' he said in between gritted teeth. Bethany smiled. This was going to be fun.

'HAHAHAHA!' roared Manfred. 'Did he really say that?'

'He really said that,' chuckled Amelia. They had all finished their meals now and were just chatting for the sake of chatting. Bethany had kept her mouth shut since that last comment and the other two appeared to have forgotten all about her rudeness. But she had her eye on a predicted meteor shower at quarter past eleven tonight so she was going to have to make an excuse to flee sooner or later. She decided sooner was probably more convenient.

'Dad,' said Bethany, politely. Manfred stopped chuckling.

'Yes, Bethany?' he replied, narrowing his eyes.

'I brought something down that I thought Ms Garcia might really like to see.'

'What is it?'

'Well, Butler said that you said that Amelia's favourite colour was yellow' – Amelia glared at Manfred – 'so I just thought…I thought she'd like to see my yellow wedges.'

'Where are your yellow wedges, sweetheart?' asked Manfred, pleased that his daughter was finally being polite.

'Oh, they're just here,' said Bethany, bringing her shoes out. Manfred smiled and then realised something.

'But…They're the shoes you came down in!'

'I know.'

'But that means…grrr…BETHANY!!!' But Bethany was already halfway up the stairs, her bare feet slapping on the cold marble floor. She ran into her room and slammed the door shut. She threw the yellow dress onto the floor and lay on her bed, giggling.

'Oh God,' she said after she'd stopped laughing. 'That was actually pretty funny.' She ran a comb through her hair and pulled on her best and most normal Mickey Mouse nightie, before leaning out of the window and letting her white-blonde hair fly in the breeze. It was ten past eleven. Five more minutes. She waited patiently for a little while longer until a streak of gorgeous silvery-white fire flitted across the sky. Bethany leaned out further, desperate to see the world outside of LA and Hollywood. She was surprised she could see anything because of all the light pollution but she wasn't complaining. After a while, she took a deep breath and sang a small lullaby that her mother used to sing to her.

For all that yelling and grumping that she did, she had a really soft voice:

*If you're feeling lonely, if you're feeling shy*
*Just throw back your head and look up at that big night sky*
*You'll see a thousand asteroids, the stars are shining bright*
*You'll know that I'll be here for you, all day and night*
*You'll always be safe and sound in my arms*
*You see that sky and you know that*
*I'm always where you are*
*You'll see that sky and know I'm where you are.*

Bethany gulped down a sob. 'I wish,' she whispered as a meteor flew past. 'I wish…I wish that there was more to my life than this.' One last meteor zipped through the darkness and Bethany crawled into bed, hoping that her wish would be answered.

Bethany woke up early. She just had a weird feeling. She wasn't sure what it was but it was weird. It was light so that meant it mustn't be too early. Bethany stretched and yawned and walked over to the window. As she pulled back the curtains, she realised why she felt weird. There was a note on her window in an unfamiliar handwriting. She was about to screw it up and go and get dressed when she noticed what the first line was. She read it through and almost had a heart attack. How could they have known? Who *was* 'they'? She read it through one more time:

*Bethany,*

*You want your life to be 'more than this'? You want an exciting existence? Then meet me at the ice sculpture festival at Polney's ice rink in New York. Don't worry, your father won't know a thing if you leave as soon as you have read this. There is money for a flight to New York in your closet along with a brand-new passport, if necessary. You're welcome. If you have no desire to meet me, then shred this note immediately. I don't need them knowing who I've spoken to. You have until midnight. I hope this helps with your wish.*

*Yours,*
*FL.*


Bethany frowned. She didn't know anyone who lived in New York, though lots of people, namely fans, might know where she lived. But how would they get in? Bethany had shut the window last night, and locked it. The person had said that her father wouldn't know a thing. That was what tempted her. Anything else and she would've shredded it and grit her teeth and gotten on with it. But this guy (or girl) seemed to know a lot. About her. She decided that she would go and raced into her closet. As she had been told, there was an open passport with Bethany's name on it and a small envelope. Inside, was several hundred dollars in notes. More than enough to get to New York. She packed a small bag of stuff, including a photo of her mother and Bobby and shoved it into a bag. She put on a white short-sleeved tee and a pair of short dungarees with a pocket at the front so she could shove the money in there. She then put on her favourite jacket, the camouflage one with a hood so she could hide her face. Finally, Bethany skipped through the door and down the stairs and ran to the lift before anyone noticed. As she ran out of the lift, she didn't even bother to say goodbye to the doorman. This was the opportunity Bethany had been longing for and it had come three and a half years early. She wasn't going to be hanging around here anymore. She ran down the street with her hood up and luckily nobody recognised her and asked for her autograph. She ran straight down to the taxi station and then hesitated. They'd ask her for her name. She quickly opened up her passport to find the words "Bethany Rosetta Hill" slowly fading out and being replaced with "Ellie Katherine Jones" appearing instead. Her eyes were wide and she was seriously considering going back home what with the high levels of weirdness but her curiosity won out. Bethany booked herself a taxi and in no time, she was standing in the airport. A flight attendant helped her get a ticket with American Airlines and she was soon on her way to New York. She sat on a row of two all by herself which was fine by her. There was no music on board but the person behind her was playing *Welcome to New York* by Taylor Swift. The skyline appeared beneath her and she was shocked to see how beautiful it was for a city. There were so many towering skyscrapers everywhere and the lights illuminated it like a light show. It looked like a model city from up above but as the plane started to dip, Bethany appreciated how large the Manhattan skyline actually was. Now this was the city to live in. No more LA, no more Hollywood. It was either here or home. And here it seemed pretty good. The plane landed with a bump and Bethany unclicked her seatbelt. She ran to the door – and drank the whole sight in. Welcome to New York…

New York was one of the most fun experiences that Bethany had ever had. She took one of those famous yellow taxis and told the driver to take her to Polney's ice rink which was apparently on 8$^{th}$ Avenue. The driver gave her a funny look but didn't seem to notice who she was. She got out at the ice rink which was bustling with people. She wasn't sure whether she should start asking around for anyone with the initials FL and so she just wandered in because it looked like it was free. There were any number of beautifully made sculptures, though it was an odd place to meet someone. Some of them, you could definitely give the title 'abstract'. She almost knocked one or two over but she managed to right them just in time. Bethany was such a klutz; it was bound to happen at some point. She was just wandering around aimlessly until someone tapped her on the shoulder.

'Oh!' she yelled, and she felt everyone's eyes on her. 'Umm…Do I know you?' The person was a he and he wore a white tee like Bethany's, with black jeans and what looked like a purpley-blue cloak thing around his shoulders. He smiled.

'No,' he said. He had an English accent. 'But I know of *you*. Know of your wish.' Bethany's eyes widened.

'You…How—? Why—? Who—?'

'Yes, I'm sure you have lots of questions. But since you're here, you'd better come with me.' He led her outside to a limo which looked very out of place on the road.

'Before I let you in, before I tell you anything, you have to agree to one thing. You have to promise, no, swear that you'll work with me.'

'But why?'

'Like I said, I can't tell you.' Bethany considered. It all seemed a bit suspicious. But she couldn't get a flight back home. This FL had only given her enough cash to get here. Obviously on purpose.

'Alright,' she said, hesitantly. 'I'll do it.' She was sure it would drag her into something much larger and more dangerous later on, but now was not the time.

'Good,' he said, a cold smile spreading across his face. 'I suppose I should tell you who I am now.' He climbed into the back of the limo and Bethany scrambled in after him. He looked at her with eyes just as bright and cold and blue as hers.

'My name,' he said, 'is Finneas Lebowski. It's a pleasure to meet you, Bethany.'

# 11. Jack Frost

Finneas had known from the very start that he wasn't a normal person. Not by any accounts. He had been raised in Germany at the foot of a mountain in a snow resort and so spent a lot of his time hiking. Accidents were common. He would walk into a certain area and a blizzard would start up. He would cause avalanches. And when he got home, everyone would yell at him. His older sister, Gertrude. His older brother, Alfred. His mother. Not his father, though. He would only shake his head. And Finneas would sit alone in his room wishing he could be roaming the mountains with his dog Bingo. He would read American comics (his mother was English so he could understand them) and try his best to resist the temptation to rip them up. He felt sorry for the bad guys. They always got beat up, kicked around and sometimes even killed. It wasn't fair. Then he'd go to school the next day and tolerate the nasty glares that every child was giving him. He was angry all the time. Being the youngest sibling, he was picked on at home as well as at school. But instead of putting up with it, he always fought back. Always threw the first blow which meant he was the one who got into trouble. He wondered why it had to be *him* that was called a devil child, the one who could call the snow to do his bidding, the one who glared and scowled at even the kindest of old ladies.

Then one day, he received a holographic message. Finneas had been thirteen at the time and was fascinated by the sci-fi contact method. A girl named Andromeda had told him to meet her at the lake that was close to his resort, at night-time. He would have ignored her, but she told him a lot of things, things that explained the accidents. And he wanted to find out why it was him. He felt no care towards the girl, just wondered why it wasn't some other unlucky child. So, he packed some of his things and left at ten o'clock. His family would notice his disappearance but they could put it down to 'missing in the snow – never found again'. Andromeda had met him at the lake with an enormous hovercraft with the words *Shadow 4* engraved on the side. She had told him everything. Finneas remembered being thoroughly baffled at the whole "Elements" concept, no matter how much it did explain. He was confused at why he was the only one at the Mansion, until Andromeda had told him the others weren't ready yet. And though he excelled at everything, though he had all the attention, he was constantly irritated. Two particular assistants got on his nerves; the blonde one, Lauren and the brunette one, Twiz. There was no one else to keep him company so Andromeda instructed them to follow him around. They did. It had been horrible. He knew he only had to wait until he was sixteen and then they would set him free. And he might've made it. But the last straw had been the final year of his time there. Two of the elements, fire and water had been orphaned and Finneas had been totally forgotten about. Andromeda and the other deity, Flare, had been so absorbed in their job trying to find new homes for them, that they weren't concentrating on Finneas. And so, he had used that opening to escape. He snuck out with his belongings and pulled together a bit of money; slowly rebuilding his resources until he had a 'villain's lair' and numerous henchmen. The only thing he had been lacking was an assistant.

And then, one night he had what he assumed was a vision of sorts. A vision of the actress Bethany Hill leaning out of her window, whispering, 'I wish my life could be more than this'. Finneas knew immediately that Bethany was the one. She had no purpose for life currently, she wanted a more exciting existence and she even *looked* perfect for the job. He wrote her a handwritten note, being careful not to give himself away and sent one of his henchmen to deliver it. He had never been more tensely anxious for someone to receive something in his life. Finneas had been expecting Bethany to keep the cash and the passport but leave the note and completely ignore him but she had arrived just where Finneas had planned. He was elated. Once he had told Bethany his name and that her father just believed that she was at boarding school, he began the long, difficult explanation that he liked to call 'the story that nobody wanted to tell'. She asked lots and lots of questions but in the end seemed to get the gist.

'So…You're the element of Ice,' she said.

'Correct,' replied Finneas.

'And all the other elements are not on your side and are in all ways and means evil.'

'Oh, they're not evil, Bethany. They are the most pathetic goody two shoes you'll ever meet and I hope for your sake that you don't meet them.' Bethany nodded slowly.

'And you want me to be your assistant.' Finneas smiled. The word probably had an entirely different meaning to him than it did to her.

'Yes, I do,' said Finneas.

'Okay. Where do you…This is going to sound really lame but…Where do you live?' asked Bethany.

'I'm sorry, Bethany but I can't tell you. As much as I trust you, if those idiots in the Mansion of Night ever get a hold of you, then you won't be able to tell them anything. They can do what they want but if you are innocent then they can't kill you. So, when we get out, I'm afraid I'll have to blindfold you. Better safe than sorry.'

'Better safe than sorry,' agreed Bethany. They drove for a long time, but Finneas' chauffeur knew where he was going. They made it to an out-of-town private airfield that was owned by one of Finneas' many spies dotted around the world. Bethany was holding out her hands like she was trying to resist the temptation to pull the blindfold off. The chauffeur opened the door and Finneas led Bethany over to their new mode of transport. Finneas sighed contentedly. He was very pleased with himself for stealing the *Shadow 4*. He had only been fifteen at the time and it was one of his major achievements. Andromeda must have got her lousy engineers to make her another one because he knew how much she liked her hover-ships. She probably called it *Shadow 5*, so predictable that girl.

Finneas helped Bethany into the ship and as soon as the doors were closed, he took the mask off. She looked around, blinking, and said, 'This is one helluva…What even is this?'

'It's a hover-ship,' grinned Finneas, showing his too-white teeth. 'Not the most modern, but definitely a close second.' Bethany nodded.

'Where'd you get it?'

'I stole it. From that girl called Andromeda. It was hilarious.' Bethany frowned.

'You make them seem so bad and it doesn't actually sound like they're doing much wrong,' she said.

'That's because if you knew *my* story then you'd realise that they're not as good as you might think. You mustn't have any sympathy for them.'

'Can you tell me your story?'

'It's too long,' replied Finneas. 'Besides, at the speed we're going, it won't take us long to get to—to our destination.' He mentally slapped himself. He'd almost given his location away and if that kind of information slipped, then Andromeda would find some way of making him spit it out. Finneas made Bethany put the blindfold on again, just in case, as the *Shadow 4* descended into his palace. It wasn't much of a palace though. Parts of it were still being built so at the moment it looked a bit like a skeleton but when it was finished it would look magnificent. The roof closed and the door slid open. Finneas hopped out and helped Bethany down too. She instinctively took off the mask.

'Whoa,' she breathed. Finneas was glad she was impressed. This whole place was designed to impress. It had a massive vaulted ceiling and was made entirely out of a glass-like blue and white substance. It looked like it had been created from crystals. The *Shadow 4* was in the middle of the room and a dozen or so of Finneas' henchmen wandered around organising what was known as the 'landing room'.

'This place is…It's…It's…I don't even have any words for it,' whispered Bethany.

'I'm glad you like it,' said Finneas. 'But I'm not going to show you around until tomorrow. I want to give you a while to mull everything over. Harold!' he yelled at a nearby minion.

'Yes, sir?' he asked.

'Take Bethany to her prepared quarters.'

'Yes, sir!' he said and then gestured at Bethany.

'I'll see you in the morning,' said Finneas. Bethany nodded and then went to follow his minion. Today had gone much better than he'd expected. He now had an assistant in training which is what he had been needing for two years. He smiled happily at his achievement and then sloped off to his own private quarters. He didn't need anyone to show *him* the way. He knew this place back to front and front to back. He knew every diamond statue, every secret crystal pathway, and every glass corridor. And yet he also knew that it wasn't enough for him. He needed the ultimate victory, the prize that every villain or villainess wanted, desired more than anything else. That night, he slept more soundly than he had slept in over two years.

Finneas was waiting for her. He had sent one of his men to go and collect her from her room at precisely ten o'clock in the morning. He was now waiting on a balcony that overlooked the main entry hall which was rarely ever used. He heard a tapping sound behind him and saw Bethany smiling as she walked down the corridor. She was wearing the clothes, the uniform, that Finneas had left there for whomever intended to acquire it. Her corn-silk hair floated around her face like a blonde cloud, and her light blue eyes sparkled maliciously. She looked like a devil disguised as an angel. Perfect.

'Good morning, Bethany,' said Finneas, his dark blue eyes glinting with hers.

'Good morning…Should I call you master? Or can I just call you Finneas?'

'Just Finneas is fine. I'm happy you're here.'

'How come?' asked Bethany. Finneas twisted his lips into a cold smile. He had been waiting for this day.

'Come, Bethany,' he said. 'I have a lot to show you.'

# 12. The Icicles

Bethany was very much at home in this supernatural world of elements and evil Ice people and flying in hover-ships. Her wish had been answered. Her life had now escalated to a whole new level. And what an exciting level it was.

Her room was enormous. Finneas had said that though the walls looked like they were made of Ice, they were actually constructed from glass. And he'd said she would become accustomed to the cold, that her love for Ice would grow. She wasn't entirely sure what that was about but it sounded alright to Bethany. Her bed had heaters in it and was lovely and toasty and the walls didn't even melt. She had a wonderful closet; a whole new wardrobe and she could wear what she liked. Still, when she arrived there was a set of clothes already waiting for her. A white long-sleeved tee, white leggings, a white cape with golden buckles and a pair of black boots, which she guessed was her uniform. There was also a jet-black face kerchief with silver streaks hanging on her wall. She had no idea what she would use that for but she didn't want to be rude and ask. The man who brought her had said to meet Finneas at the main entry hall at ten o'clock in the morning but she had had to ask someone to take her as she hadn't a clue where it was. He had been waiting there for her with a glint in his eyes and a smile on his face.

'Come, Bethany,' he said. 'I have a lot to show you.' Bethany followed him down corridor after corridor, his words about how it had been built, and its architecture floated over her head. She was too busy staring at everything. It was like snowflakes; from a distance, it all appeared the same, but if you looked closer, each wall was unique in some way. A slight swirl in the glass wall that was different, a shimmering statue or a frozen and eerily silent fountain marked each room as different from the others. He showed her the dining room; a vast room with a waterfall on one wall, rushing and gushing behind a sheet of clear ice. He showed her the control room, where all calls were received, where all the technology was located. He showed the not-yet-finished sculpture room which was little more than a building site presently. He walked down hallways that seemed endless. It was all amazing but all the same for Bethany. Until Finneas spoke up and said, 'Through here, this is the most important room in the whole palace.'

'What is it?' asked Bethany.

'Well, you know how everyone wants something greater in life?' Bethany snorted.

'You can say that again.'

'Well, what *I* want…At the risk of sounding like a cartoon villain…I want control. I want power. Everything, Bethany. And you're going to help with that.' Bethany gulped. She had expected something like that but it hadn't hit her yet what the actual scale of it all was.

'But to get power,' continued Finneas, 'you need an army. An army of followers to do your bidding. I have discovered a way of getting that army.' He pushed open the door in front of them. It opened onto a viewing platform. Bethany very nearly choked. It looked like that scene from *Star Wars*: the one where the clones were walking about and being put together. Only these were no clones. These were hundreds, no, thousands of different, separate people. The majority of them were dressed in white outfits with white masks that covered their faces. Just like all the other henchmen. A small caged off area in the corner of the cavern contained some very bored looking boys and a girl who was asleep. Bethany's eyes widened.

'Explain,' she whispered.

'Well…These people are what I refer to as 'Icicles'. People who obey me and only me. I select people from all over the world who have special talents. That boy there, he's a black belt in karate. The girl has one of the highest IQs in Europe. All of them are smart or violent in some way.

'I take them and I offer them an ultimatum: agree to work with me or…Well, or else. If they agree, then I give them a non-exponential share of my powers, they will have powers that never grow. They will stay mortal but will live their life as an Icicle. Those who disagree…They have second and third chances, but those who disagree can be…Disposed of.'

'Disposed of,' whispered Bethany.

'The Icicles are knitted out for my true intent: world domination. I plan to turn the world into an Ice Age, and those who surrender to me will live in my sanctuary. Those who don't, will meet the same consequence as everyone else. The moment I have enough Icicles, I will unleash them onto the world and they will force the citizens of every country to surrender. But I know of some monsters who will stop me.'

He reached out and touched Bethany's cheek. A cold sensation numbed her face but she couldn't move away from him. Her feet were rooted to the spot.

'I just gave you the mark of Ice, the symbol of growing elemental power,' said Finneas. 'You will grow to become as powerful as me. I gave you the mark for a reason.

'Those rats in the Mansion of Night are sure to try and stop me. In some way. It is your job to…get rid of them. Give them the ultimatum—surrender or—' Bethany stopped at that point. Her heart was racing. Something felt different. She felt…cold. But it didn't bother her.

'You!' she yelled. 'You can't do this! It's inhumane! It's…Not right!' Finneas' face didn't change.

'I signed up to work for you. That's fine. That's cool. But I did *not* sign up to…to…to…'

'The word assistant,' mused Finneas, 'has multiple meanings. It could mean my lieutenant. Or it could mean…My assassin.' The words lingered in the air. A tear slipped from Bethany's eye and it froze on her cheek. 'I can't…I can't…' she stammered.

'You will,' said Finneas, harshly. 'I don't care how or when you do it but you will.' He turned his back to Bethany. She ran out of the door and kept running until she found her quarters. She stood in the middle of the room and surveyed it. She looked at the desk and saw what the computer displayed. It was a document labelled: OPERATION ICICLE. She read through the names, looked at the photos. She brought her eyes to the bottom of the paper. It read: Operation Leader—. And a blank space. She knew she had pulled herself into something she shouldn't have, she knew she'd swam too deep. She was drowning. But she also knew that if she didn't do as Finneas had asked, then not only would it be them, it would be her. The cursor was next to the word 'leader'. Bethany's hand hovered over the keyboard. She pressed the letter 'B'.

# 13. Unprepared

The definition of "epic": Sky Alisa Calling. Or at least, that's how it was in Sky's head. She was acing training and was thoroughly enjoying even the easy courses, but every time she saw that huge grey ocean, she knew she could beat it but it brought back the memories of her first time on the course. She had created a bubble of air around herself that acted as an air pocket but that had very nearly burst. Scary. She had attempted to fly over the fires in the second chamber but they were too high so she was forced to blow them out. Difficult. The third test hadn't been so hard, she easily flew over the void. The fourth test, she had tried to both fly over the maze and find her way through, but both attempts had failed and so she had gotten angry at the maze. Looking back, she felt a bit stupid. Oh, hindsight is a cruel thing. And then, the fifth test. The one that sent Rico into fits of laughter every time she mentioned it. Sky had walked straight into the glacier; that bit was enough to make Rico giggle. Then, when she realised that she would have to scale the glacier using only a rope, she yelled, 'Are you kidding? You're kidding.' She had gotten halfway and then shouted, 'Darn you, glacier! Go to hell!' That bit made Rico double over hooting which earned him a thump on the back and a stern glare. But now, she could look that challenge in the face and grin. Nothing in that course could beat Sky Calling. The only thing she hadn't quite mastered was the agility course which looked a bit like a climbing frame that had been working out. She was still at the falling off stage on that one.

So, of course, that was the course that Sky was determined to conquer. She would make herself look away from Harvey and Rico wetting themselves on the side-lines and concentrate on the monkey bars or the aerial hoops but even Andromeda's voice was beginning to sound strained when she was encouraging Sky. But she would not give up. She would conquer or die of embarrassment. At the moment, it was looking like the last option.

'You can do it!' yelled Andromeda. 'Thirty more seconds! Keep going!' Sky fell off the monkey bars. Andromeda sighed. 'Or, we can do it again.' Sky got up and dusted herself off. Harvey grinned at her.

'It's a good job we didn't bet on you doing this. I would've thought you'd be able to do it a month ago.'

Sky wrung her hands. 'Shut it, dirt boy. Or a stray breeze may just pick you up off the floor and ram your head into tomorrow.' That made Harvey laugh more.

'Cut it out, Harvey. She's trying,' called Andromeda walking over. 'It's not like you're a professional either.' Harvey stopped laughing. That would've made her feel better but Rico walked over.

'Here it comes,' muttered Sky.

Rico was still snorting and wiping the tears off his face, but in between snuffles he managed, 'Hey, Sky. Are you just doing that for our entertainment? If so, please carry on. I am entertained.' Rico might be entertained, but Sky was *not* amused. She was about to make a comment about how she might be bad at the agility course but she wasn't half as terrible as he was at styling his hair, but a *beep* from the far side of the room caught her attention. Gwen walked out of the doors and wiped the frost from her hair. She took one look at Rico snorting and Sky glaring and immediately gauged the situation.

'Give her a break, Rico,' she said as she walked over. 'I don't know why you're pestering her. I would've thought you'd be watching Bertie Mila.' Rico blinked and then frowned.

'You didn't tell me the surfing championship was on.'

'I didn't want you to lose concentration on the training,' replied Gwen. 'I also didn't want you to hide in your room for a week, crossing your fingers that Bertie'd make it through to the finals. Your obsession with that girl is ridiculous.' Sky and Gwen shared a smile. Rico had a small crush on the Australian surfing star which used to be annoying but now was a good weapon to use against him.

'Why didn't you tell me?' he cried. 'I thought you liked me!'

'I do,' said Gwen. 'But if you wanna watch it, I suggest you flee. The first competition will be halfway through if I checked the times right.'

Rico's eyes widened. 'I'll…um…be off then.' He scarpered up the stairs and back to his quarters.
Harvey grinned. 'Oh, the joys of being thirteen,' he scoffed. 'Yeah, right.' Andromeda smiled weakly. 'Just be glad that you actually *have* an age,' she said. 'Being age*less* is not as appealing as it sounds. Trust me, I should know.' Sky wondered what it must be like, living eternally. As much as

being young forever sounded great, what did you actually do with your life? The only people Andromeda could meet were the elements and hers and Flare's assistants. Sky considered what Andromeda had said. She decided to use it as a quote someday.

'So, what are you planning on doing now?' asked Gwen, breaking Sky's thoughts. 'I'm gonna go sit with Rico to make sure he doesn't tear his hair out.'

'I am going to smash this agility course to pieces,' Sky said. 'I'm sure I wouldn't hurt its feelings.'

'I'm watching Sky fail—I mean I'm going to cheer her on,' added Harvey, coughing. 'She could do with the extra encouragement.'

Gwen rolled her eyes. 'See ya then.' Sky waved back and then sighed.

She rolled up her sleeves and growled, 'You will *not* defeat me. I will not die by the hands of a climbing frame.'

Harvey laughed. 'The climbing frame is beating you, Sky. You need to up your game.'

Sky glared at him. 'You wanna try being me?'

'I'm good, thanks.'

'Didn't think so.' She walked through the middle of Harvey and Andromeda who reluctantly brought out her stopwatch.

'You have two minutes,' she said, like every time. 'Ready?'

'As I'll ever be,' murmured Sky.

'Three, two, one, GO!' Andromeda's words echoed around her, as she sprinted towards the first obstacle: a springboard. She leaped onto it, willing the air to help her up. Her hands caught hold of the rope and she latched her legs around it. She felt like an elemental Ninja Warrior. From the rope, she jumped to the floor and felt the spongy mat beneath her trainers. She lifted her arms up and wrapped her fingers around the metal monkey bar. This is where she had failed before. She looked down and her glasses slipped off her face. 'Drat,' she muttered. Now she was even *more* likely to fail. She reached out her other hand but it just felt thin air. She reached out too far and…

'OOWWWW! My foot!' she yelled, clutching her toes. It didn't feel broken but it was definitely sore. Harvey and Andromeda ran over.

'You okay?' asked Harvey leaning over her.

'Do I LOOK okay?'

'Nope.' Andromeda got down on her knees and touched Sky's trainer with one finger.

'It's not broken,' she said, looking up. 'But it's gonna sting for a while. Dark Healing is not the most caring way to heal someone, but it's efficient.' Sky stood up and attempted a few steps. She could walk, but she was limping.

'Thanks, Andromeda. Least I can—what was that?' She had been about to say, 'Least I can walk' but she had been interrupted by a quiet rumbling sound.

'Thunder?' asked Harvey.

'Maybe Flare has a stomach-ache,' suggested Sky. Andromeda shook her head.

'Neither,' she said. 'Flare and I don't eat. And, anyway, I know that sound.' She balled her hands into fists and then looked up, a scared expression on her face.

'That's the *Shadow 4*! But…Oh no. Oh God. TAKE COVER!' she yelled and darted towards the stairs. At that moment, the ceiling burst into a thousand tiny fragments.

# 14. The Kidnapping

The first thing Gwen heard was the rumbling. A groaning sound like Twiz driving a hovercraft. Then Andromeda shouted 'TAKE COVER!' and a smashing sound filled the air and she knew something was wrong.

'Rico,' she urged. 'Let's go.' They ran out of Rico's quarters and into the Hall of the Elements and came out in the main area of the Mansion of Night. Twiz was standing on the centre of the bridge with a frightened expression on his face.

'What the hell was that?' he asked, as Gwen and Rico ran over.

'No idea,' said Gwen, hoping that her idea was wrong. 'But if it's enough to make Andromeda scream, then I suggest we run.' They ran down the spiral staircase and onto the bottom floor.

'Come on,' said Twiz. 'They won't think to look in our place.' He led them to a small corridor that looked similar to the Elemental Quarters. There were doors everywhere, each with a name above, and he led them to a door labelled 'Twiz'.

'Get in,' he urged. 'I'll go find Lauren.' And he ran off leaving Gwen and Rico alone.

'Did he just desert us?' asked Gwen. 'How rude.'

'I wish he'd stayed,' said Rico. 'I wonder what's out there?' There was a loud humming sound that came from nowhere in particular and it was making Gwen's ears hurt. It was definitely a hover-ship but not the *Shadow 5*. It was too loud to be that; the *Shadow 5* was silent as a whisper. Gwen's heart was racing, and she suspected who it might be. Someone who wanted revenge on the elements. Someone evil. Someone who had a hover-ship. Someone Lauren had told them about one month ago. Suddenly, there were voices outside and Harvey staggered into the room along with Twiz and Lauren. Rico stood up.

'Where's Sky?' he asked. 'And Andromeda?'

'Sky's still in the hall, hiding,' said Harvey. 'Andromeda's tryna' hold them off but…'

'But what?' asked Gwen, her heart sinking.

'I dunno. But when she blasted them with darkness, a blue light came from them and the blast went thinner and thinner and…It might be gone.'

'We've gotta help her,' said Rico. 'You coming, Gwen?' Gwen didn't want to leave the safety of Twiz's place, but Andromeda was in trouble.

'Of course.' And so, they ran back out of the assistants' quarters, back up the stairs, back through the Hall of the Elements. They burst through the door and ran to the top of the stairs. What they saw was not pretty.

Andromeda was in the centre of the room, her hair swirling wildly, a grim expression on her face. A pulse of black light was streaming out of her hands, pushing off a similar white pulse. The white energy was radiating from a hover-ship that was almost an exact replica of the *Shadow 5*.

Yells were coming from inside the open door: a girl's voice 'But I thought you said—'

A boy's voice, 'I know what I said. Changes have to be made. He could be very useful. We have to try.'

Rico surveyed the scene and began to run down the numerous stairs. 'We gotta help!' he yelled. He realised he wasn't quick enough and so he leapt into the air. At that moment, the yelling from the hovercraft stopped abruptly and a blue pulse shot out just in time to hit Rico full on. He froze in mid-air and fell to the ground covered in frost. Gwen was horrified. No one did that to her brother.

'Nooo!' she shrieked, taking the stairs two at a time. But it was too late. Rico was floating up towards the hovercraft, frozen as he was. Gwen ran over to Andromeda who fell abruptly to her knees.

'I…can't…' she whispered and closed her eyes. Gwen joined her on the floor and watched through streaming tears as the hover-ship ascended through the gaping hole in the roof. Twiz appeared at the top of the stairs and when he noticed his mistress unconscious on the floor, he almost fell down the stairs in his hurry. Gwen whispered one word before the world turned upside down, 'Rico.' That was the last thing she registered before she blacked out.


Gwen woke up freezing. She was lying on the floor in the training hall with four intent faces staring down at her: Harvey, Sky, Flare and Lauren. Gwen noted that Twiz was missing but that was not her most prominent problem.

'Rico…Where…' she managed. Harvey grabbed her arm and pulled her into a sitting position. Sky held her glasses in one hand and dabbed at her eyes with the other. Lauren was sniffling. Flare looked mortified.

'I'm sorry, Gwen,' he said, his usual swagger had deserted him. 'You were just in the wrong place at the wrong time. We had no idea that Finneas would attack us. If we did, we would've transported you to America or something. I'm sorry,' he said again.

'It appears that he has gained himself an assistant,' said Lauren, miserably. 'Ever heard of Bethany Hill? She dragged herself into something much too dangerous for someone like her.' Gwen nodded, but she wasn't really listening. She was just grasping the situation: Rico was gone. Maybe not permanently, but gone. She asked a question to get the dread off her mind.

'Where's Twiz?'

'He's with Andromeda,' said Sky. 'She was…What was it called again?'

'Drained,' said Flare.

'Yeah, that. She was drained. She was sucked dry from her powers and they just need time to grow back. But what about you? You okay?'

*Apart from the fact that my other half has just been kidnapped, yeah I'm fine*, she wanted to say. But she didn't want anyone to be as upset as her so she said, 'Yeah. If you mean physically, I'm fine. Mentally, I just want to curl up and cry. How long was I out?'

'Not long,' answered Harvey. 'Bout three or four hours. You look better than before. Your eyes were all red and horrible.' He smiled but it was quickly replaced with a pout.

'Is there any way to get him back?'

'We're already on it,' said Flare. 'Biggle is leading the search on the location device and Jupiter was out scouting as soon as we told him.' Gwen nodded.

'Can I see the location device? I might be able to find a pattern.' said Gwen.

'Sure,' said Flare. 'It's worth a shot.'

# 15. Jack Frost Makes a Call

Harvey was watching Andromeda pacing the control room. He had never seen anyone so irritated in his life; her face conveyed no anger but if you looked into her eyes, you saw that she was impossibly irate that Finneas had had the nerve to steal Rico. It would've been funny except for the fact that Harvey wanted to be up there pacing with her. They were all desperate for the locator to start showing some useful data. Gwen had tried to find something that might give them a clue where he was but it didn't work. She had then kicked it and burst into tears. Andromeda had tried to contact her search party but with no luck. Emelie was being a nuisance and not answering any calls so who knew what they were up to. Jupiter had told them that they were currently searching the Scottish Highlands but to no avail. Biggle was very frustrated that his device wasn't working properly. And Flare was so on edge, he yelled at Lauren accidentally and made her cry. The atmosphere was tense on an extreme level.

They had all been floating around the Mansion and the Palace for roughly three days now, waiting expectantly to hear the news that Rico had been found but it didn't happen. Often, at night, Sky would go over to Gwen's quarters and they would weep together. Harvey wanted to go too but he wasn't sure Gwen would be happy with him turning up and asking if he could come in. So, he cried alone, in the dead of night, when nobody would hear him. He would stare at the photo of the "gang" that had been taken a week after being found by Andromeda. He would toss and turn and try not to let anything bother him but after a while he couldn't stand it. He decided to go up onto the roof. Unfortunately, he forgot what Lauren had told him about not going up there in case he found Andromeda conversing with the darkness. He was halfway up the ladder when he heard crying and someone saying, 'It's my fault. I should've stopped it. I should've killed that blasted…I…I…I am useless.' Harvey didn't get to the top of the ladder.

Now, looking at Andromeda walking back and forth, he felt a surge of pity. She must be beating herself up over everything though it was no one's fault but Finneas.. And Bethany's. He never would've thought in a million years that Bethany Hill, that gorgeous actress, would go evil. He felt no affection towards her now. He just wanted to shove a rock in her face. Squish her nose. Let his anger loose. He was barely keeping it together and was only doing so for Gwen's benefit. He looked across the room at Flare who was shaking his head.

'I'm sorry, guys,' he said, glumly. 'I can't take it.' He trudged out of the room, raking his fingers through what little hair he had. Andromeda stopped briefly and then went back to pacing. Sky took off her glasses and rubbed her eyes.

'Coward…' she muttered, half-heartedly. All of a sudden, a screen went blank. It flickered and then turned off completely. Everyone stopped what they were doing (which wasn't much) and stared at it.

'Biggle?' said Andromeda. 'What the heck?'

132

Biggle shrugged frantically. 'W-wasn't m-me!' he stuttered. Gwen got up slowly and walked over to it. She tapped it once and they all gasped in harmony. There, on the screen, was a smiling face and a pair of malicious blue eyes.

'Finneas,' growled Andromeda.

'FINNEAS!' she yelled running over to the screen. 'WHAT HAVE YOU DONE WITH RICO, YOU NASTY LITTLE—'

'Now, now,' said the boy, who Harvey had guessed must be Finneas. 'Mind your language, Andromeda. The boy isn't harmed. Merely a captive.'

'A CAPTIVE!' she shrieked. 'You have no right to do this! I never did anything! I trained you. I provided you with a home and food. I made sure that you weren't lonely. And how do you repay me? You steal my hover-ship, *and* you steal a trainee! How dare you, you rat!'

'Andromeda,' said Twiz, touching her arm. 'This could be a clue.'

'Right,' she said, calming down. 'A clue. So why now, Lebowski? You had two years. Why wait?'

'Why now? Because I am ready. To bring you down. To vanquish you. Rico is the bait. As long as I am sure that you will come to get him, he will not be harmed. But the second you surrender…' He paused and ran a finger across his throat. 'Catch my drift?'

'Oh, I catch it, you repulsive snow-worm,' snarled Andromeda. 'Just like I will catch you. Now, tell me where you are, so I can come and tear you to pieces.'

'Why would I do that? That would be giving the game away. All I want from you is cooperation.'

Harvey bit his lip. He wanted the personal pleasure of whacking this guy upside the head. Sky and Gwen looked like they felt the same.

'Cooperation,' murmured Andromeda. 'I'm afraid I can't do that.'

'Then, *I'm* afraid our conversation is over,' said Finneas, his cold lips twitching at the edges. 'I hope you come around to my point of view. Good day.' And the screen blacked out.

# Epilogue

Rico woke up with a throbbing headache. He hurt all over – and it was weird. It stung like he was cold, like he was freezing. Literally. His head was resting on someone's lap, a girl by the looks of it. Her blonde hair was draped over her shoulders and was tickling his face. He opened his eyes wider and saw who it was.

'Bethany Hill?' he asked weakly. 'What the…'

'Be quiet,' she hushed. 'I'm trying to brace myself.'

'Why…What?'

'You wouldn't get it.' She was right. He had no clue where he was. It looked like the inside of the *Shadow 5* but it wasn't quite the same. There was one other person in the passenger bay – a man in a big white suit with a mask across his face. He wasn't sure what that was, but one thing he was sure of: he was no longer in the Mansion of Night.

'Where are we going?' he asked.

'Dunno,' replied Bethany. 'He never told me where it was. But,' she said, 'I do know what it is called. My dear, stupid friend, we are going to the Ice Maze.'

↢**The End**↣

# Andromeda's Guide to Elemental Rules, Forfeits and Concepts

## Introduction

I know everything. I'm not showing off, just stating the truth. So, I thought I'd try and share some of that knowledge with you. Not all of it though, because you might explode like that lady from *Indiana Jones and the Crystal Skull*. That would not be funny. I do not need another unexplained spontaneous combustion on my conscience.

## Rules and Forfeits

You might think that there are lots of rules that the elements have to follow; if so, you are wrong. In actual fact, there are around the same amount as the Ten Commandments, maybe less. I like to think that the Prophecy Stone got bored and couldn't be bothered anymore so it gave up. Flare thinks that it was sparing us. I think he's wrong. I have not come across one single time when the Prophecy Stone was nice. Fight me.

## Rule 1. Elements shall not reveal themselves in any way to the eye of a mere mortal.

This one is complicated. If I reveal the mysteries of the elements on purpose, then the stone would either take my powers, my immortality or if it got up on the wrong side of bed it might just kill me. But it can only take one of the three. If, say, Sky broke this rule, then the stone could only take her powers or kill her. But never both.

If the element was revealed by another person, then that person would take the forfeit.

If the element was not revealed on purpose, but by accident, then it would go down as an accidental sighting. Take Twiz, for example. If he saw me then I would tell him everything and give him the option to either join me and become immortal or go back into the mortal world as a local loony. Most people who have had a hard time at home choose to join me but the rest put me down as a superstition, a dream. So, if you ever hear anyone banging on about a scary she-devil luring them in for the kill with her pale vampish skin and her long black hair, then you know it's probably me. He, he, he, (evil laughing).

If Gwen was spotted on the street lobbing fireballs at a building, then nothing can be done. If the witness didn't see me then I could potentially remove the scene from their mind as that is one of my special powers (see extras).

## Rule 2. Mortal elements shall have the right to create replicas but not without a notice.

This is what Finneas (that little worm) was doing. He was creating non-exponential replicas. He was giving a small portion of his power to another person, knowing that his would grow back. He could then choose whether the new replica would have exponential (growing) powers or not. Bethany is the only known exponential replica, which means she will grow to be as powerful as Finneas (great, two evil maniacs, just what we need).

### Rule 3. Elements shall be permitted to drain others but not without notice.

Draining. Ugh. The bane of my life. All elements have the power to steal the power of another element though it is deeply frowned upon. The thief can choose to expel the power into the air, meaning that it will grow back or keep it for himself, meaning it won't. I've only ever seen one element keep another's power once and they gave it back in the end anyway.

### Rule 4. Elements shall not be romantically involved in case the element of power is passed down incorrectly.

I hate this rule. I hate it, but it's necessary. I will use Gwen and Rico's parents as an example. If Gwen and Rico had not been born twins, if it had just been Gwen, what would have happened? An element with double powers? Gwen proved that one right. What if that was the only child they had? What if there were two of the same? It is just not worth the risk. I have seen this rule break many people's hearts before but it has to be done to keep things equal. Gwen and Rico (or Rick as he was called then) were a major relief. I knew from the moment they were born that something would go wrong but I didn't want to spoil things. I said zippo. I was right.

**Rule 5. If an element does not or cannot pass down their powers, the Prophecy Stone has full control of who the line will be diverted to.**

This one's easy. It doesn't really have a forfeit, it just means that if, say, Harvey didn't have any kids, the Prophecy stone would choose who got the powers of Earth next. Either that or it would keep them. Super-elemental hog.

That's it. I think. I told you there weren't many. All that's left now is the concepts, which isn't that large either.

# Elemental Concepts

**<u>Draining</u>**

See rule three.

### **<u>Marks of Power</u>**

See rules one and two.

### **<u>Magic</u>**

This might sound stupid, but how else does the Hall of the Elements expand? How else does my Mansion create another room whenever I acquire another assistant? Magic…

That's it for that too. Now for my special extras.

## Extras

### **<u>1. Mind Wipe</u>**

I can remove certain people and scenes from people's memories, provided the person hasn't seen me. In that case, I'm stuffed.

### **<u>2. Appear and Disappear</u>**

I can make things appear and disappear. I gave Sky and Harvey the cash to get to the correct destination; I took their possessions, added the hologram, then gave them back; I made sure I had Maryanne and Richard's rings so I could give them to Gwen and Rico.

### 3. Memory Wipe

Slightly different from a mind wipe. I can erase certain memories and insert new ones; that is how I convinced Rico and Gwen that they weren't related, how I made them believe the Italian couple were Rico's parents.

### 4. Photo Erase

Good grief, that's a lot! I can make people disappear from photos, but not appear. Bibbidi, bobbidi, boo.

### 5. The Vortex (last one)

I can make a sort of portal for the hovercraft to travel through. Cool, huh?

Anything else, I haven't discovered yet. I think I have extras and Flare doesn't because I am as old as eternity, whereas Flare is only as old as the Big Bang (ha ha-dee ha ha!). Still a helluva long time to put up with someone though. Anyway, that's it. I hope your knowledge has improved somewhat; if not, let me know so I can give myself a time out.

Kidding!